FOSTER

By JESSICA ASHE

Dedication

Thank you to everyone who helped make this book possible. I won't name any names, but you know who you are. I wouldn't have been able to do this without you.

Chapter One

FOSTER

I'd lost her.

Where had she gone? She was beautiful and fully deserved the opportunity to place her lips around my cock later tonight.

Somewhere in this room of lawyers and other equally boring people was an absolutely stunning young woman who'd caught my eye while I'd been stuck talking to one of the partners at my firm. By the time I'd ended the conversation, she'd disappeared.

I cast my gaze around the room, but couldn't find her. Still, there was plenty of time and I only needed ten minutes to work my magic. Better make that fifteen. Women at networking functions always took a little more effort, and you had to pretend to be interested in their careers first.

When did I become one of those lawyers who went to networking events?

Lawyers and potential clients mingled and partook in the weird dance that was professional networking, talking to people for long enough to get a business card and know whether they might be any use.

This gathering was hosted by one of the large law firms right here in downtown Washington, D.C. I hated these events, but I had to get my name out there, and this function was so close to my office, I'd be an idiot to miss it.

Nearly everyone here was in their forties, apart from the eager looking young attorneys desperate to further their fledgling careers by sucking up to some of the partners. There were even a few law students milling about hoping to make connections and land a job to help repay the six figures of debt they would have on graduation. I didn't envy them, but that didn't mean I could be bothered to help them either.

I needed a drink. I headed to the bar and settled for a European lager. It was either that, or a cheap-looking wine. The firm could easily have paid for better quality, but they didn't want people having too much to drink. Serving shitty wine was a subtle way of making sure the guests limited their intake.

A fellow M&A lawyer from another firm had cornered one of my old law school buddies and was currently boring him senseless with talk of all the deals he'd closed recently. I knew he would rather do anything other than talk about work, so I decided to help him out.

"Tom, how are you doing?" I said loudly, shaking his hand and thrusting myself between him and the partner. The relieved look on Tom's face as we made small talk made it clear that he was pleased to see another human being and not just a robot.

"Thanks for that, Foster," Tom said, as the old partner wandered off without so much as a business card to show for his efforts. "Are all these events so fucking boring?"

"Pretty much," I replied. "I don't go to many, but I never find lawyers much fun to drink with. Even in law school the parties were dull."

"Speaking of law students, there's a fair few of them here tonight. No doubt they'll approach you at some point and kiss some ass. I just had some smarmy little junior associate from another firm try to act like he's a partner. He must only be a year or two out of law school."

Both Tom and I had moved so quickly up the ranks that we forgot we were only five years out of law school ourselves. It felt like we'd been lawyers for at least a decade.

"Speaking of entitled brats," Tom said, as he flicked his head to the side, motioning to a young attorney in an expensive suit. "That's the one. Try to stay away from him if you can."

I thanked Tom for the advice, but I didn't need it. The kid stood out from a mile away as being some rich jackass who probably got a job at daddy's firm. Okay, so I worked at my mom's firm, but that was different. I wasn't a slimy little prick like this kid, for one thing.

"He's got a face you just want to punch," I remarked.

"I miss the good old days where we used to go out and get in fights instead of staying in and studying."

"It's a miracle we ever got admitted to the bar."

I kept an eye on the young associate as he walked around like he owned the place, in a suit that looked way too expensive for someone who should still be paying off law school loans. I tracked him with my eyes as he walked over to the bar. He turned back with two glasses of wine and handed one to a young blonde in the corner of the room.

The young blonde. It was her. The one I'd spotted earlier.

She was fucking beautiful. If we were in a bar, she'd have hundreds of men hanging off her every word. It said something about the crowd here that no one else seemed to have noticed her, except the slimy guy now trying to chat her up.

Screw networking; I needed to have a bit of that. Her long, blonde hair draped teasingly down her back, just begging to be pulled on in the throes of passion. She broke out into a forced smile at what was probably a bad joke from the kid, but fake or not it still lit up her face.

I needed to see those lips wrapped around my cock.

She wore a knee-length skirt, but I could see enough of her ass to picture the scene as I yanked up her skirt, tore down her panties, and went to town on that pussy. I wouldn't quite have described her as petite, but she was definitely on the slim side and her breasts protruded from her frame, hugged tightly by her white blouse. I'd had bigger breasts in my hands, but hers were more than ample considering her frame.

This night might not be such a waste of time after all. She looked a little uptight, but so do a lot of women. That doesn't stop me charming the panties off them-- literally--and having them end the evening a lot more satisfied and less uptight than when they started it.

"Shit," Tom muttered. I'd forgotten he was still there. "Our IP attorney just spotted me. I'm going to have to spend a few minutes with him. I can introduce you if you like?"

"No thanks," I replied. "I have someone else I need to meet."

I pulled out my phone just to look busy, and leaned against the wall near the chick I would be seeing naked in hopefully no more than three hours' time. It immediately became clear that she already knew the entitled prick currently trying to chat her up. They could be colleagues, but she sounded deferential to him and nervous when she spoke.

Her name badge marked her as April Rhodes, a summer associate at Cooper & Cooper, and a first year law student at a nearby school. His name badge pegged him as Zach Cooper, a second year associate at the same firm.

I knew exactly what was going on. The summer was nearly over, and he'd likely been flirting with the poor girl the entire time. Now he was making his move.

"We should go out for drinks soon," I overheard Zach say. "Not at an event like this. Somewhere a little more intimate."

"I'm going to be busy once school starts," April responded. "I won't really have time for that sort of thing."

Well done. You turned him down and gave him a way to retain his pride. Now let's see if he takes the hint.

"Nonsense," Zach said dismissively. "You'll have plenty of time. Remember, the goal of going to law school isn't to get great grades, it's to get a job as a lawyer. I can make that happen."

Jesus Christ. He was a second-year associate, not a fucking partner. Except he had the surname Cooper. Ah, that explained a lot. I'd thought he looked like the type who'd landed a job with his dad's firm and I'd been right as always.

"I don't think it would be appropriate," April said, quickly changing from one excuse to another.

I didn't have a lot of experience at being rejected by women, but surely it had to be obvious to Zach that he didn't stand a chance here. Could some men really be that clueless?

"As of next week, we won't be working for the same firm anymore," Zach responded. "We can do whatever we want."

April blushed and swept a loose strand of hair behind her ear. God, she looked fucking stunning when she was lost for words and red in the face. I would have her the exact same way later on, except she'd be horizontal and not as quiet.

I'd never imagined myself getting hard in front of a group of old lawyers, but right now April had me growing in my pants, and she hadn't even noticed me yet. Or at least, she was pretending not to have noticed me. Women always spotted me in a crowded room. I stood out from a mile away, and never more so than I did right now.

In addition to being taller than most people here, I was the only one who bothered to work out on a regular basis. My large frame was impossible to miss among the combination of lawyers who either ate too little or too much. None of them exercised; it took time away from billing. April must have noticed me, but she was doing a good job of not looking this way.

"I want to work for Cooper & Cooper next summer and after law school," April said. "I can't do that if we're dating."

"You do realize you won't be working for my firm if you don't get a good appraisal from me?" *'My firm?'* Fucking asshole. "I don't want to have to tell the partners that you are uncooperative and not a team player."

Come on, April. Stay strong.

"I guess I could think about it," April said softly.

"Look, let's get out of here now," Zach said. "We can go somewhere else and have some privacy."

Zach placed his hand on her upper arm. To any casual observer it would look like a gesture of goodwill, but I could see his fingers gripping her arm with enough strength to be threatening.

There was no way I was going to stand for that, and neither was April. She tried to pull her arm away, but he held on tight.

That was all the excuse I needed.

I walked over to Zach and stood up straight, casting a shadow over him that he noticed immediately.

He turned round and looked up at me like a deer caught in the headlights.

"I'm going to give you one chance. Let her go and you don't get hurt."

Chapter Two

APRIL

Why was it guys always felt the need to flex their muscles in front of women at the worst possible times?

I was handling the situation. Okay, I wasn't doing a great job of handling it, but I'd managed not to draw any attention to my unwanted conversation with Zach. Now this towering mound of muscle was going to make a scene while he tried to look like a knight in shining armor.

I'd seen him standing nearby reading work emails. It's not like anyone could miss him. His suit was tailored to fit snuggly around his muscular chest, which was practically bulging out through his shirt. It looked like he could make all the buttons pop off just by flexing his pecs. Although I wouldn't have minded seeing that.

He hadn't bothered with a name badge, but I couldn't blame him for not wanting to put a pin through that expensive suit.

Zach still had a hold of my arm, but that didn't seem important right now. I looked up at the man until my eyes found his. They were a deep green, and they matched my gaze with an intensity that I initially mistook for passion, until I realized it was anger. His jaw looked tense and his lips were pursed, as he breathed heavily through his nose and turned his attention to Zach.

I breathed a sigh of relief as he looked away from me. Being under his gaze had been like hiding in a cupboard in a horror movie--I had to stand completely still and not make a sound or I would end up devoured. In this case, that might not be so bad.

As I exhaled, a small shiver spread from the back of my neck throughout my entire body, leaving an aching warmth between my legs. This man was bad news.

"Who the hell are you?" Zach asked, looking up at my suited knight. Zach looked woefully inadequate up against this man, but he had the arrogance not to realize it.

"It doesn't matter who I am. You need to take your hand off her arm now," the man ordered. "I'm not going to say it again."

"We were having a private conversation," Zach said, sounding slightly less sure of himself now. The man's biceps were bulging through his suit, whereas Zach's suit hung off him limply. Zach hadn't brought a knife to a gunfight, he'd brought a spoon, and not a particularly good one at that.

"Alright, if you insist," the man said. "We can deal with this the painful way. Painful for you, anyway."

"No," I snapped, finally finding the strength to speak. "I don't want to make a scene."

The career office at law school had been clear on the topic of behavior at parties and networking events--don't get noticed. Have a few drinks, but not too many. Be reserved, but not afraid to speak when spoken to. The office never specifically said don't get into fights, but I suspected that was implied.

The man put his hand on Zach's wrist and pulled the hand off my arm with ease. I saw Zach wince in pain, but he quickly hid it as he tried to salvage some pride. The man put his hand on Zach's back and pushed him towards a nearby fire escape. I cringed as the door opened, expecting an alarm to go off, but it didn't, so I followed them through. At least now we were out of sight of everyone else here.

"This is assault," Zach whined, as the stranger threw him up against the wall.

"Actually, this is battery," the stranger replied. "Don't they teach you anything in law school?"

"I'll sue you for this," Zach said. I looked down and saw that he was only in contact with the floor by the tips of his toes. The stranger had lifted him into the air, so they were close to being face-to-face.

I wouldn't have minded my face being that close to his, even if he did look rather angry right now. Angry could be exciting.

Damn it, April, calm down.

"No, you won't," the stranger said confidently. "You'll keep quiet, and we'll keep quiet about how you tried to blackmail this young lady into going on a date with you. Is that how you get all your dates, Zach?"

"That wasn't what happened," Zach said, as he tried pathetically to free himself from the stranger's grip. Why couldn't I work at a firm with lawyers like him, instead of people like Zach. Not that he would've even noticed me, but something nice to look at over lunch would've been nice.

I used the time while the man had his back to me to shamelessly check out his ass. His suit jacket covered some of it, but what I could see was more than enough to have me subconsciously lick my lips. I'd barely touched the wine, but there was definitely a chemical reaction going off in my body right now. What other reason could there be for me wanting to sink my teeth into a man's ass? I'd never even thought about that before, let alone done it.

"Can I trust you to leave the lady alone?" the man asked Zach.

Zach nodded, beads of sweat running down his forehead. The man hesitated for a few seconds and then finally let go. Zach dropped to the floor, gasping for breath, and looking like the pathetic low-life I knew he'd been from the moment he introduced himself to me on my first day in the office.

The man turned to look at me. His face was still taught with anger, but that didn't quench the passion burning between my legs.

"Are you okay?" he asked.

I nodded, brushing some hair behind my ear, even though it wasn't in my way. His face relaxed into the most perfect smile I had ever seen and for a few blissful seconds I forgot about Zach leaning against the wall, still trying to catch his breath.

"You're done for at my firm," Zach yelled.

"Ignore him," the man said. "Let's go back outside."

"You're never going to get a job. Fucking bitch."

The man stopped just as his hand was about to open the door. I felt a heavy gust of air on my shoulder as he exhaled, trying to control his temper. It didn't work.

"Sorry about this," he said, before turning round and swinging his fist hard into Zach's face.

Zach hadn't been expecting the punch, although even if he had, I doubted there was much he would have been able to do about it. His body slammed back against the wall, before he dropped down to his knees in front of the stranger.

To give Zach his dues, he didn't know when to quit. Blood poured from his mouth, but he grabbed onto a handrail and tried to stand up. The punch had left him dazed, so he promptly lost his footing. He kept a firm grip on the rail, but that just made his balance worse.

Suddenly he disappeared from view as he slipped halfway down the flight of stairs.

The man looked down at him, but made no offer to help him up. "He's still breathing," the man said, before turning his deep green eyes back to me. "You want to get out of here?"

I nodded. I wanted to go wherever he was going.

Chapter Three

APRIL

I'd had plenty of one-on-one meetings with lawyers over the last year, but none like this.

My law school recommended reaching out to lawyers and offering to buy them coffee for the chance to get to know what they did on a daily basis. Of course, the point was to impress them and hope they'd offer you a job or at least a more formal interview, but we all went along with the charade.

This meeting was different. We'd already knocked back a couple of drinks each and now I was hitting that stage where the alcohol had removed my usual inhibitions and brought me dangerously close to flirting. That was bad because I couldn't flirt. I was hopeless at it even with men I knew and trusted. With this guy--what was his name?--I didn't stand a chance.

I'd been quiet at first, but now he couldn't shut me up. I'd told him all about Zach and how he had used every opportunity to get me in his office over the summer. Zach had put himself in charge of my assignments, so everything I did had to flow through him.

He'd insisted on going through all his corrections in person, usually sitting next to me and peering down my top as he pretended to point out my mistakes.

"You could report him," the man said, as he came back from the bar with another drink. How many was this? Three? Four? It was too many. I shouldn't be drinking so much in front of an attorney. It wasn't professional. "Law firms don't want to deal with claims of sexual harassment."

"His dad's a partner, so that isn't really an option. Besides, I don't want to get that label. I'll never find a job if I'm the one who files sexual harassment claims during a summer job. Not that it matters now. I'm screwed. Zach's going to make sure I don't get invited back next summer."

"You sure you want to work there anyway?" he asked. "Working in a big law firm isn't all it's cracked up to be."

"It's all I've ever wanted to do," I responded. The man frowned, clearly thinking it odd that I dreamed of working for a big law firm.

I unloaded on him. I couldn't help it. I'd blame the alcohol, but I'm not sure it was that. There was something in his eyes that made me weak, and stripped down the barriers I usually kept in place for professional conversations.

I didn't even know his name, but I told him how my mother had been a lawyer for a big firm and how I wanted to follow in her footsteps.

"What does your mother think about this?" he asked.

"Not a lot. She died seven years ago."

"Sorry. I know how you feel though. My father passed away a few years back."

"You don't need to hear all this." I closed my eyes and took some slow breaths. I was starting to sweat under my clothes, but I didn't know if that was because of the heat or the sight of the man opposite me.

"Let's go up to the roof," he said, taking me by the hand and leading me upstairs.

It wasn't any cooler outside. The humidity in D.C. tended to last well into the evening, but at least there were fewer people out here. We found a spot in the corner with a degree of privacy. I took a slow sip of my drink, using it as an opportunity to stare at him again. He had a thick neck with a visible vein, which weaved between muscles that I hadn't even known existed.

I'd been drinking with this man for over an hour now, and all I'd done was make myself look like an idiot. Other women were looking in our direction, like vultures waiting to pounce once he'd realized I wasn't worth it and decided to move on. The least I could do was make a bit of effort. I mumbled something about feeling hot, and opened a few buttons on my blouse.

I instantly regretted it, when I saw a flash of the tatty old bra I'd slipped on for the evening. Hardly a great impression to make, and it's not like my tits were worth showing off anyway.

"I'll make sure you get a job next summer," the man said. "But it won't be where I work."

He looked down at my exposed chest, without bothering to be subtle about it. Usually I would make a quick attempt to cover up, but instead I crossed my arms under my breasts and pushed them up slightly. Maybe it wasn't too late to salvage something from this evening.

"We don't take summer associates at my firm," he continued, looking up into my eyes again. I thought I caught a glimpse of desire there, but it quickly disappeared. "No offense, but they're not worth the hassle."

"Oh, thanks," I replied, in mock indignation.

He smiled and once again a flush of heat washed over my body. This one definitely had nothing to do with the humidity.

"You did well to get a job in your first summer though," he said. "How did you manage that?"

"Good grades, I guess."

I was being modest. I had near perfect grades, but I didn't want him to think of me as some nerdy law student right now. *Why did I have to wear such a boring skirt?* I tried to subtly pull it up, but it refused to budge, staying firmly put around my knees.

"I hope you find the time for a little fun once in a while," he said. "I partied a lot in law school. Makes all those cases a lot easier to bear."

"I'm not really the partying type."

"There's nothing like just letting go for the evening and having the time of your life."

"Have you settled down now?" I asked.

"Is that your way of asking whether I have a girlfriend?" he asked, flashing a smile at me.

"Just curious."

There was no way he had a girlfriend. He looked every bit the playboy, in his expensive suit, and the devilish look in his eyes made it clear he wasn't exactly after a girlfriend or anything even remotely serious.

"I don't do relationships. If I'm feeling particularly generous, I will spend an entire night with one woman and give her an experience she'll never forget, but that's it. The most anyone gets is one night."

I raised my hand to my mouth, but I wasn't quick enough to cover the laugh that escaped my lips. I don't know why I found it funny. I just hadn't been expecting him to be so forward. Or so boastful. One second we were talking about work, and the next he was telling me he was some sort of sex god. I believed every word he said.

"Are all lawyers this arrogant?" I asked playfully.

"Yes," he replied. "But *I* have the goods to back it up." He leaned in, and for one terrifying second I thought he was going to kiss me, but he just whispered in my ear. "If you want to check out my goods, you can go right ahead and reach out a hand. In fact, better make it two."

He was worse than Zach, except this time I didn't care. I should leave now, go straight home and forget all about this stranger, but I knew I couldn't. I was physically incapable of looking away from him, and even if I did make it home, I'd never be able to just forget him. There wasn't enough alcohol in the world for that.

I didn't reach out like he wanted me to, but I did look down. Even in the dim lights on the rooftop, I could make out a substantial bulge between his legs where he brazenly had his erection on show for anyone to see. Except only I could see it. The erection was for me; all I had to do was claim it.

"What makes you any better than Zach?" I asked, trying to ignore the fact that my heart was beating furiously in my chest.

"I'll make you come," he responded without skipping a beat. "A lot. You'll still be screaming my name in ten years' time when you're married with kids. I'll take you in ways you've never even dreamed about. What would Zach do? Squirm around on top of you for a bit while you pretend you're enjoying it?"

I laughed again. That was probably an accurate enough description, if not of Zach then certainly of some ex-boyfriends of mine. Most of my ex-boyfriends in fact.

"How far away do you live?" he asked.

"It's about a ten minute walk."

"If we leave now, I can have you coming in twenty minutes. You'll be soaking wet, and come will be dripping down the insides of your thighs and pooling on the bed."

Holy fucking shit. He meant it.

25

This wasn't some idle talk. I could actually be in the throes of an orgasm in twenty minutes' time. The thought was paralyzing. I hadn't come with another man since I started law school.

"Looks like I have an answer," he said, smiling and nodding down at my chest.

My nipples had stiffened, and the worn padding of my bra had done little to help hide the evidence from appearing on the front of my shirt. We were both visibly erect; there was no denying that we both wanted to do this. The only question was whether we should.

Screw it. I needed this. I needed him. It's not like I would ever see him again.

"Okay then. Your twenty minutes starts now."

Chapter Four

APRIL

The walk back to my apartment took a lot less than ten minutes, largely because the man--God dammit, what was his name?--moved at twice my usual pace, and I had to hurry to keep up with him.

We entered the dingy, old apartment building located just a fifteen minute walk away from school. The place was "cheap," which in D.C. meant anything under $2,000 a month for a one-bedroom apartment. All in all, it was the perfect place for a broke student. It *wasn't* the perfect place to bring home a one-night stand which you were hoping to keep a secret.

The man pressed the button to call the elevator. As usual, only one of the damn things was working and it appeared to be stuck on the eighth floor.

"What floor are you on?" he asked.

"Fourth."

"We're taking the stairs," he said, grabbing my hand and pulling me towards the stairwell.

"What's the rush? Worried you won't meet your twenty minute target?"

He stopped and turned around, pushing me gently against the wall. For a second, his eyes latched onto mine, and then suddenly his lips covered my mouth, enveloping me in the most passionate kiss I'd ever had.

I placed my hands on his shoulders, not really sure what else to do with them, and then surrendered myself to him. His reached down and tugged my skirt up enough so that my legs could open wide enough for him to slide between them.

His erection pressed against my stomach, until he lifted me off the floor and let it rub teasingly against my sex.

Suddenly I heard the loud metallic sound of a door opening above us. I tried to push him off me, but for a few seconds he resisted, pushing his large cock against me one last time, before letting me go. I only just about managed to pull my skirt down by the time Colin, from my section at school, bounded down the stairs.

He looked far too awake for this time of night, which probably meant he was up consuming ridiculous quantities of caffeine--the drug of choice for most law students.

"Evening," I said nervously as they approached. My 'date' just stood there grinning, loving every second of my embarrassment.

"Hey," Colin responded. "I'm just off to the shop for some study provisions." By 'study provisions' he probably meant disgusting energy drinks, if the empty cans that usually littered his apartment were anything to go by. "You want anything? Or do you have other plans for the evening?"

Colin had a well-deserved reputation as a gossip. Within a few days, everyone in my section would know that I had brought a man home from the bar and I would never hear the end of it. You could get away with one-night stands in college, but everyone in law school thought of themselves as far too mature for that kind of thing. Usually I was one of those people.

"This is my brother," I said, motioning to the stranger and hoping to God that Colin hadn't come around the corner quick enough to see us kissing. "He's in town for a few days, so he's going to crash on my floor for a few days."

"Nice to meet you," the man said, giving Colin's hand a firm shake. "I'm going to have my head down on April's carpet within minutes."

Oh my God, way to be subtle.

"There are no carpets," Colin said. "Just hardwood."

"No carpet?" the man said, flashing me a smile. "That's just fine with me."

Colin didn't seem to notice the obvious innuendo, so he just carried on down the stairs and out the door.

"Brother?" the man asked. "It's going to be rather hard to explain all the screaming coming from your room, and trust me, there's going to be a lot of screaming."

A gentle shiver spread down my spine as I remembered his promise. *I'll have you coming in fifteen minutes.* We didn't have long if he was going to keep that promise, but I knew he wouldn't need it. My panties were wet from the brief moment he had his erect cock rubbing against me. If he touched my exposed body... I shivered again.

"Let's get upstairs," I said. "We don't want to bump into anyone else."

And I want to get you in my bed, I thought as I turned toward the doorway and went inside.

I led the way up the stairs. I could feel his eyes staring at my ass the entire way. Just thinking of the things he would do to me once the door was closed had me feeling weak at the knees, like I was trying to climb the stairs after a long run.

We headed onto the fourth floor, and down to the end of the hall to my apartment. I fumbled around in my purse for my keys, but I could swear they were hiding from me, as if giving me one final chance to back down and tell this stranger to go home. There was no way that could happen now. I didn't want it to.

My hand froze in my purse, as I felt his breath on the back of my neck. His lips brushed lightly against the soft skin, as his hands reached around and cupped my breasts, which felt tiny in his grasp. Perhaps that was why I usually went for smaller men--so as not to feel quite so inadequate.

"Do you want me to open the door or not?" I asked, as I sank back into his rough embrace.

"If you don't do it soon, I'm going to knock the door off its hinges."

I didn't doubt him for a second. The keys gave up hiding, and I pulled them out of my purse, my hand shaking from fear, excitement, or both. I heard the man growling behind me as I fumbled with the key, not getting it in the lock until the third attempt.

The key finally slid inside.

I opened the door and the man immediately pushed me through, slamming the door shut behind me. This was it. I had a stranger in my house for the first time ever. This was going to happen.

His hands went straight to my blouse, opening the buttons with surprising dexterity given the size of his fingers. This wasn't the first blouse he'd removed in a hurry, but I tried not to think of that. His experience in these situations was the very reason I had invited him back to my apartment; I couldn't hold that against him now. We were going to fuck, not get married.

My blouse had barely hit the floor, when his hands pulled down the zipper on my skirt and tugged it past my thighs before letting it slip to the floor.

He examined me in my underwear, while he was still fully clothed. We'd have to rectify that soon. I wanted to see what lay under that suit almost as much as I wanted to take his attention away from my tatty old bra and panties.

"Where's the bedroom?" he asked, his breath heavy with desire. "We can do this here, but I prefer a bed to work on."

I pointed to the room on the right but let him lead the way. He took a firm hold of my hand and pulled me through the door, before pushing me down onto the bed. I still felt exposed, so I tried to get under the covers.

"No," he said sternly. "I want to look at you."

I laid back on my elbows and tried to look confident as he gazed down at my body, taking in every inch of my skin. When he looked between my legs, I felt certain he could see through my panties. He probably could--they were soaking wet and the white fabric would need peeling off my sex.

"The clock's ticking," I said jokingly. "You don't have long left."

"I have plenty of time," he replied. He wandered around the other side of the bed, and finally slipped off his suit jacket, placing it on the back of my chair. His thick fingers removed the cufflinks from his shirt sleeves which he placed on my desk. He sure was taking his sweet time.

"It's only fair that I get to see you naked too."

"You will," he replied, as he slowly started to undo the buttons on his shirt. As the shirt opened, I saw the tattoos spreading from his chest up to his arms. I'd never been with a man with tattoos before--this really was a night of firsts in many ways. I couldn't make out any particular pictures on his chest. There just seemed to be a black swirl of lines and shapes covering his upper body.

When the shirt fell to the floor, my eyes followed the markings to his arms, and traced them all the way down to his wrists. The tattoos had just about been covered by the shirt he wore. I wondered how many of

31

his colleagues and clients knew what he looked like when the suit came off.

Plenty of women had been in this position before me, and there would be plenty after, but the way his eyes remained focused on me as he undressed made me feel that right here in the moment I was the most important thing to him. At least I would be for the next hour, anyway.

He'd taken his pants off while I had been staring at his chest, and now he was walking up to the bed in just a pair of boxers that did absolutely nothing to hide the stonking great big erection bursting through, straining to be let out.

I should be terrified right now, but there was just enough alcohol still in my system to make me giddy with excitement instead. He sat down on the bed next to me, and reached behind me, flicking open my bra in one quick movement, and then pulling it off from the front with his other hand. He'd done that before.

My nipples were already rock hard, and my breasts were now covered in goosebumps despite the warmth in my apartment. He looked at them greedily, then lowered his mouth as if to kiss them, but instead went lower, kissing my belly button.

He crawled between my legs, as his kisses went lower and lower, finally touching the cotton of my panties. I reached down and slipped my thumbs under the waistband, desperate to get them off and have him touch my pussy, but he stopped me, grabbing my wrists and pushing them away.

"Not yet," he said softly. His lips went to the inside of my right thigh, where he kissed every inch of exposed skin.

I whimpered under his touch, and moved my sex towards his face, desperate for him to move faster. For a man who had only a few minutes left to make me come, he certainly was taking his time.

Finally he flicked his tongue against the damp cotton between my legs. I let out a low groan, and looked down at him. Our eyes met. He wanted me as much as I wanted him. His thumbs hooked under the waistband of my panties, and I lifted my ass into the air, ready for him to whisk them off. Instead he moved his mouth to my left thigh and resumed kissing me, seemingly oblivious to how much my pussy needed to feel his touch.

Usually it was me trying to slow guys down, hoping to stretch out the experience, but now I couldn't bear the wait. Each kiss sent a tingle of heat through my body, but I was already hot where it mattered. Hot and wet.

Once his lips had touched every part of my inner thigh, he raised himself up on his knees and looked down at me. I couldn't look at anything other than the massive bulge between his legs. I didn't even care about him going down on me anymore. I was already wet enough. He could just take me now if he wanted to, and from the look on his face, I was fairly sure he did.

His fingers took hold of my panties, and this time he did pull them off before casting them to one side and heading back down between my legs.

I raised my hips to meet his tongue, desperate to get him touching me as soon as possible. He immediately took hold of my legs and locked me in place, stopping me from moving.

"I'm in control here," he said sternly.

"Then get on with it," I yelled in frustration.

He smiled. "You know, I could just make you wait. I have all night."

"Don't you fucking dare," I replied. "Do you want me to spread the word that you broke your promise?"

"Good point."

He lowered his lips between my legs, and finally his tongue darted out and slid between my folds. I gripped the bedsheet and cried out as if in shock, but I couldn't move my legs. He had me locked down and completely under his control.

His tongue explored every crevice, circling my entrance, before moving up to my bud, which was now swollen and sensitive to tough.

This man wasn't full of empty promises. He'd meant it when he said he could have me coming in minutes. Already the sensation of his touch had completely overwhelmed me, and my inability to move just heightened the desire. Every muscle in my body had tensed up, as he greedily lapped up my juices. I was only seconds away from coming hard in his face.

Then he stopped.

"Keep going," I whimpered. "Please."

He looked down at me with lips and his chin covered in my essence, but then stepped off the bed. He picked up his pants and for one fearful moment I thought he was going to leave. Perhaps this had all been some twisted joke to get me close and then leave me to finish the job myself.

Instead I heard the distinctive sound of a foil wrapper being torn open. When he came back to the bed, his large cock had been freed from its cotton prison and was sheathed and ready to go.

"I want you to come all over my cock," he said, matter-of-factly. "I want to feel your tight pussy clamp down on it as you come hard while I fuck you."

I knew that was going to happen. It wasn't even up for debate. The only question was how long it would take. If I were a betting woman, I'd place my money firmly in the 'less than two minutes' category.

He climbed back between my legs, and lowered his lips to kiss me. I tasted my eagerness on him, as I pressed my lips to his, waiting impatiently for him to enter me.

"It's been awhile, hasn't it?" he asked.

I nodded, as my breath quickened in anticipation. Surely it would happen any second now?

"You've never had it like this before," he said, as his hands reached up and firmly squeezed my breasts. "And you never will again. You only get me for one night."

If even half my brain had been properly functioning, I would have thrown him out for being such an arrogant asshole, but all it did was make me want him more. Some cocky people are assholes. Some cocky people are just right.

I only had one night, so I was done wasting it.

"Hurry up and fuck me," I whispered in his ear.

He moved his hips and suddenly he was entering me. His fingers parted my folds, and his tip slipped inside. I screamed as he pushed himself all the way inside. For half a second, I worried about what my neighbors could hear, but that thought disappeared with the second thrust.

"I never took you for a screamer," he teased.

"I'm not usually."

"I do tend to have that effect on women."

"Stop talking and keep fucking," I demanded, not wanting to hear any more about his performance with other women. I was trying to keep those thoughts as far away as possible.

He responded with harder and deeper thrusts, sending my back shooting up into the air as if I'd just been electrocuted. I groaned loudly, digging my nails into his back as he did exactly what he'd promised. My pussy acted just as he'd predicted. I tightened around his cock, and came hard, letting the wave of euphoria rush over me.

The stranger stiffened while I was still catching my breath, and by the time I had opened my eyes he was rolling off of me, having emptied himself inside the rubber sheathing his large cock.

He kissed me passionately, before getting up and throwing the condom in the trash. We didn't speak. We both knew it was pointless. He wrapped his arm around me, and I closed my eyes, drifting off to sleep moments later.

At some point during the night I woke up--or he woke me up--and we went at it again. This time in the dark. It was slower, but still aggressive. He tugged at my hair, as his cock filled me with each powerful thrust.

I lost count of how many times we both came. The last one might have been a dream. I couldn't even tell anymore. But he'd been real. He'd left behind a note to prove it.

I like souvenirs, so I kept your panties. F

Of all the things we did last night, the part that left me most embarrassed was knowing he had that tatty old pair of my underwear. He'd peeled them off me last night when they were dripping wet, but now they were probably in a pile along with countless other pairs far more flattering than mine.

I couldn't think about that any more. I'd had my one night of fun. He'd promised an orgasm and he'd delivered. More than once. He'd also promised it would only be one night, and it looked like he intended to keep that promise as well.

I hadn't realized just how much I'd needed that. I hadn't had sex since starting law school, so that made it nearly a full year. And the last time had been a fumble with an ex-boyfriend. Hardly earth-shattering. Not like last night.

But that was it. My mystery man had given me a good night, and now I had to get on with my life. I had bigger problems than worrying about some stranger I'd never see again. Last night's events had likely messed up any chance I'd had of working at Cooper & Cooper next summer. If I wasn't careful I would finish law school in debt *and* unemployed.

The stranger had helped solve one of my problems last night, but he wasn't about to offer me a job. It was sex, not an interview.

He was a stranger--a mystery--and if I knew what was good for me I'd keep him that way. Because one thing was certain; he was also bad news.

Chapter Five

APRIL

Eight Months Later

I'd been blacklisted. I was only a second year law student and word had already gotten around the local law firms that I'm not to be trusted.

Way to go April. Your mom would be so proud.

Cooper & Cooper never technically sacked me. They let me work out the last week of my summer associate position, but on the last day I was summoned to the human resources office and told in no uncertain terms that while my work had been satisfactory the firm would not be offering me a position for my second summer.

I'd stupidly assumed that I would be able to work for Cooper & Cooper during my second summer in law school as well, but obviously that couldn't happen now. All the other big firms had already met their recruitment needs, so that left me still looking for work in May when there were no jobs left to take.

I was completely fucked. And not in the good way. Not like the stranger had fucked me eight months ago.

Shit. What was that? Three hours without thinking about him? Not bad I suppose. The only time I made it much longer than that was when I was sleeping. Even then...

Stop it, April. That ship has passed. You had your one night of fun, and now it's time to live with the consequences. The main one being that you have no job for the summer, and will have to hope for a miracle to land a job after law school.

The legal market for new lawyers was cutthroat. If you didn't have a good job in your second summer then you probably wouldn't have one when you graduated. Those were the cold hard facts. No amount of good grades could change that.

I'd always wanted to work for a law firm. That's what my mom had done when she was alive, and it was my dream to do that same. However, at this stage I had to explore all possibilities and that meant meeting with the only lawyer I knew outside of Cooper & Cooper.

Well, Bryan wasn't the *only* lawyer I knew, but I didn't even have the stranger's name. He might not even be a lawyer for all I know. He had the arrogance of one, but those tattoos, they hadn't been typical of a lawyer. Neither was the way he'd fucked me.

Bryan met me for a coffee at a cafe near the Department of Justice where he had worked since graduation. He didn't get paid anywhere near as much as lawyers at law firms, but then he didn't have to work the same crazy hours either.

"How did exams go?" Bryan asked, after he'd bought a couple of coffees for us. He was only two years out of law school, so he still remembered the sheer horror that came over law students around this time of year.

I shrugged. Exams didn't seem important any more. I was in law school to become a lawyer and get a job as one. What good were grades if no one would hire you afterwards?

"Exams aren't the problem," I replied.

"No job still?"

"No job."

"What happened at the last place? You did so well to get a job for your first summer. Not many people manage that. What went wrong?"

"There were a few issues between me and other attorneys. One attorney in particular."

Bryan raised an eyebrow. We had been friends before either of us had even started law school, but now he was the lawyer and I was just the law student. It probably wasn't appropriate to tell him all the details. I hadn't told anyone about Zach except... *him*.

"I know how clever you are," Bryan said, "so it can't be anything to do with your work."

"I had a row with a second-year associate. That associate happens to be the son of the managing partner."

"Ah. That would certainly be a problem. Do you want to work for the Department of Justice then? I assume that's why you called out of the blue for a meeting? Not that it's not great to see you of course."

"I'll be honest, at this point I would take anything. I don't mean that to sound rude or ungrateful, but it's the truth."

"I'll see what I can do," Bryan said unenthusiastically, "but I don't fancy your chances. This year's summer intake was sorted a long time ago. They're already reviewing resumes for the next summer."

I sighed, but just managed to resist the urge to bang my head on the table like I did at home when frustration got the better of me. "I figured as much. Thanks anyway."

"How're things with your dad? Last time we spoke you said things were a little awkward."

"They're okay," I replied. "He's dating someone and he wants me to go home for the summer and meet her. That's another reason why I want to get a job." My phone vibrated on the table with an incoming message. "Speak of the devil."

"I'll leave you to it," Bryan said. "I'd better be getting back to the office anyway. I'll keep an ear to the ground, see if anything comes up."

"Thanks Bryan."

Dad wanted me to call him. That meant another lecture about spending more time with him and meeting his new girlfriend. God, it felt weird to even say that. My dad was officially doing better at this whole dating thing than I was.

I knew I should be more grateful for him. He wasn't trying to shove a new mom in my face; he just wanted me to meet the woman who was making him happy. Losing Mom should have meant I cherished Dad even more, but all it taught me was that even those who love you unconditionally can still disappear from your life at a moment's notice. It had been a brutal life lesson.

I picked up my phone and called Dad while I still had the energy to argue with him if need be.

"Hey, Dad," I said cheerfully. "What was it you wanted?"

"Just wanted to see if you could come home next weekend?"

"I'm still looking for a job. I can't afford to take the weekend off from my job hunt."

That was true enough. Applying to the big firms was the easy part, but none of them had even responded with a form rejection letter. Now I was hunting around looking for jobs with smaller firms.

They didn't have dedicated human resources departments and navigating their websites to figure out the application process took a lot longer than tailoring my resume and cover letter to whatever practice area they covered.

"So, if you were to get a job in, say, the next week, you would be able to come home for the weekend?"

"Well… yeah, I guess so. But I don't even have an interview lined up at the moment, so that's not likely."

"I have a feeling things are going to turn around for you real soon," Dad said, with his typical optimism.

As far as Dad was concerned, I could do no wrong. He was also convinced that I would get a great job because "what firm wouldn't be lucky to have you?" He didn't know how badly I'd messed up last summer, and no matter how many times I'd told him the legal market sucked right now he wouldn't listen.

"If a miracle happens and I get a job then I will definitely travel home and meet this new lady friend of yours."

I'd have to meet her at some point, but I'd rather do it when I had a decent job in place. The way Dad described her, she sounded like a successful businesswoman, and I didn't want her looking down on me as a failure.

"I'll see you next week then, sweetie," Dad said confidently.

"Don't get your hopes up, Dad."

"What can I say? I just have a feeling that things are going to work out."

"Bye, Dad."

I placed my phone back down on the table. Barely a minute passed before it vibrated again, this time with an email. I almost ignored it--assuming Dad was emailing me a job posting that he thought I was suitable for--but I hated having unread email messages. The little red circle on my email app drove me absolutely nuts.

The email wasn't from Dad. It was from an administrator at the law firm of Arrington & Hedges.

Dear Ms. Rhodes,

Thank you for your interest in a summer associate position at Arrington & Hedges. Your resume was of interest to a number of the attorneys here, and we would therefore like to invite you to have a formal interview.

As I'm sure you can appreciate, time is of the essence, so please give me a call at the number below and we can arrange a time that is convenient for both of us.

Regards,

Melissa

I immediately called Melissa and arranged an interview for Friday afternoon. She gave me a list of the three partners I would be interviewing with and that was it. Just like that, my mood had gone from miserable to jubilant.

For once, Dad's confidence in me hadn't been misplaced. There was just one thing that didn't sit right with me. I started browsing the website for Arrington & Hedges to get a better idea what areas the firm practiced in--mainly corporate law with some tax and litigation work--and then it hit me.

I'd never applied to Arrington & Hedges.

Chapter Six

APRIL

Over the last six months, I'd given my contact details out to upwards of one hundred attorneys, so it was possible I had met a lawyer from Arrington & Hedges at some point and just forgotten about it. However, a firm like that would never take a summer associate on just because I happened to meet one of their lawyers at a networking event.

There could be no doubt about it; I had been blessed with some phenomenal good luck. Now I just had to get through the interview. Or rather *interviews*.

I'd been given twenty minute slots with three different partners at the firm, one right after the other with no time to stop and collect my thoughts between them. That was probably for the best. My thoughts were a mess of nerves, with an unhealthy dose of fear. The less time I had to think the better.

Two of the partners were corporate focused, while the third an employment litigator. I could impress the corporate partners easily enough with my background of doing similar work last summer and the corporate law classes I took in school.

The other partner would be harder work. I had to pretend to be interested in employment litigation so as not to appear rude, while also making it clear that I didn't want to do that kind of work long term. Most lawyers were cool with that, but you always got the odd one who took it as a personal attack if you didn't want to follow in their footsteps.

Arrington & Hedges' office took up the top three floors of a large building just a block from where I'd been working last summer. There weren't many firms that were more prestigious than Cooper & Cooper, but this was one of them. They didn't even bother with a summer associate program, which was why I'd never formally applied there in the first place. I guess this year they were making an exception.

I smiled as I walked past the comparatively dingy building that housed Cooper & Cooper, and strolled into the Arrington & Hedges' building, hoping against hope that Zach happened to be looking out of his office window at just that precise moment.

I shouldn't get ahead of myself. The job wasn't mine yet, but I knew I had a good shot. Big firms didn't let law students take up an hour of time from three partners unless they had a shot at a job. An hour of partner time at this place was worth nearly a thousand dollars. I was costing them money just by being there.

The receptionist greeted me with a smile and told me to take a seat. The career office at law school always hammered home the importance of leaving a good impression on everyone at the office, and that very much included the receptionists. It's not like I'd planned to be nasty to her, but apparently some students walked into law firms with a self-important attitude, and job opportunities had been lost after bad reports from office staff. I knew a fair few students like that. In fact, most of the students I knew had that kind of attitude.

Not all lawyers were bad. My mom had been a perfect example of that. She'd been a hot-shot partner at a law firm in New York, but she'd never let it get to her head or affect her relationship with me and Dad. She'd come home late quite a lot, but she'd always found time to put me to bed or just chill out for some mother-daughter chats when I was older.

I'd taken her for granted, as all kids did with their parents, but now that I'd started law school I had a better idea of how difficult it had been for her. She'd been the breadwinner. Dad earned money, but not a lot. He worked hard, but a security guard's wages didn't go far. Mom had been the one to buy the house in upstate New York, and pay for me to got to private school.

The reception area had recently been remodeled to have a minimalistic and modern look to it, however that was par for the course in large law firms these days. Each firm had to look the part, and expensive artwork helped justify the massive fees these places charged.

As with Cooper & Cooper's offices, only the reception area and meeting rooms looked glamorous. An assistant collected me and led me to the first partner's office. Last year I'd been surprised at how low-key all the offices where, but now I knew what to expect. Office space was expensive in D.C., and there wasn't a lot of it. You took what you could get.

The partners earned millions a year, but the three that I met didn't have large corner offices, and judging by the files and books piled up everywhere it looked like they could have done with the extra space.

I found the mess relaxing. It was good to know that the people interviewing me were human as well. I didn't trust people who claimed to be busy while keeping an immaculate and tidy office. There was something highly suspicious about that. Even when I just had one project on the go at a time, I still filled out all the space I had with legal textbooks, printed out cases, and client files. At least that way no one questioned whether or not I was working.

Each of the three interviews followed a similar pattern. After some basic pleasantries, the partners had started to appear disinterested and one of them admitted that hiring a summer associate was unusual for the firm. An exception was being made just for me, and I had no idea why.

When things threatened to get awkward, I used the research I had done on my interviewers to ask them pertinent questions about recent cases they had worked on. Even though every law student did the same thing before interviews, the tactic never failed to impress, and the partners took the bait, talking about themselves until well past the twenty minutes of allocated time.

I didn't relax until I was out of the third and final office, and heading back to reception. I felt like I was walking on air, and not some thin, worn-down carpet. Even though the offices themselves weren't impressive to look at, I found it impossible to imagine I would be back here in a few weeks for a summer associate position. This place was too good for someone like me.

I was nearly out the door when the receptionist called me back. "Ms. Rhodes, there's been a late addition to the interview list. You're to meet with Mr. Foster Arrington as well."

Arrington? He was a named partner, so he must be important. I wouldn't be meeting with him unless I had a decent shot at the job, but I had to make a good impression.

"Do I have time to do some quick research?" I asked the receptionist. I figured she wouldn't mind me being honest about why I needed the extra time, and that way I might be able to do it on the spare computer next to her instead of on my phone.

"Actually, you're to go through straight away," she said. "Mr. Arrington has a meeting in fifteen minutes, so it needs to be quick." It *would* be quick if we didn't have anything to talk about. "Just take a right and go all the way down to the end of the hall."

"Thanks," I said, forcing a smile. This is where everything had the potential to go dramatically wrong. Some people could just wing it in interviews and sound impressive. I was not one of those people. I needed notes--bullet points of what to say beforehand. Without them, I was just a law student sitting there like a deer in the headlights.

No one paid any attention to the stranger wandering down the hall. Mr. Arrington's door was closed. I pressed my ear to the door to make sure he wasn't on a call, but I couldn't hear anything. I knocked gently, but didn't get a response.

I knocked louder, but managed to sound angry and aggressive. Not quite the impression I was going for.

"Yeah," the voice said from the other side of the door. "Come in."

I straightened my skirt, and made sure my blouse was still tucked in. I didn't feel as fresh as I had done before the three interviews, but I told myself that he wouldn't notice any difference. Besides, the managing partner was a guy, he'd only notice my outfit if one of my nipples was showing.

I walked in and shut the door behind me. Mr. Arrington didn't even bother looking up from his monitor. He didn't need to.

I'd recognize that body anywhere. Those shoulders were unmistakable. I'd seen them every night when I closed my eyes for the last eight months.

"It's you," I said, dropping all pretense as he looked up at me with those deep green eyes.

"Hello April," he said grinning. "How lovely to see you again."

Chapter Seven

FOSTER

It's her.

She must have tracked me down. I never gave her my name, but my photo was on the law firm website. She must have looked up every lawyer in D.C. until she found me. I had myself a stalker.

A beautiful stalker.

A beautiful stalker who'd been the best sex I'd ever had.

April stood there in a skirt and blouse exactly as she'd done that night at the networking event eight months ago. She looked professional--like a law student dressing as an attorney--but I knew what lay underneath that blouse and skirt.

The blouse was tight enough to show the outline of her chest, but it didn't do justice to what lie beneath. I could still picture those perfect, small--but firm--breasts in my mind as clearly as the night I had held them and sucked greedily on the teats.

It had been a damn good night, I couldn't deny that. But I still hadn't gone back for more. I never went back. One night only, that was the rule. If you gave a woman more than one night of pleasure then before you knew it they were leaving a toothbrush at your apartment and you were shopping at Bed, Bath, & Beyond together on the weekends.

I knew from experience that women often wanted more than one night with me, but the feeling was rarely mutual. In fact, it had never been mutual.

But April had been... special. I'd been tempted to look her up; it wouldn't have been difficult to find her, but that way lay commitment.

"What are you doing here?" I asked sternly. "This is a law firm, you can't just show up in my office."

"Are you kidding me? You made me come here."

"This isn't a joke. You can't be here."

If you are going to be here you could at least do me the honor of bending over my desk so I can get another go on that tight pussy.

"I was told to come to your office," she snapped. "You must have summoned me here. What's the matter? One night wasn't enough for you?"

I shook my head to clear my thoughts. I'd had similar conversations with women before, but usually it was the other way around.

I glanced over at my monitor and saw an incoming email from Mom. *I've just arranged for a candidate for a summer associate position to pop by your office. I want you to interview her to make sure she's appropriate for the position.*

I already knew exactly what positions April was appropriate for.

"Sit down," I snapped. "It sounds like you're here for an interview."

"I might as well just leave," she replied. "Clearly this isn't going to happen."

"Stop being stubborn and sit down." *Or stay standing up so I can check out your ass if you prefer. Either way is fine with me.*

April pouted, but eventually sat down opposite me, brushing her hair behind her ear in that cute way she had done eight months ago. She was nervous.

I was going to enjoy this.

"Let's get started shall we," I said. "I only have fifteen minutes, although we both know I can achieve a lot in fifteen minutes."

"Twenty," April muttered, as if that made much of a difference.

"If you say so. Why do you want to work here?"

April sighed, and then blurted out a clearly rehearsed answer in a bored sounding voice. "The firm works with large clients, and I want to be a part of deals that make the national news, even though I appreciate my role with be small."

I hoped she'd been a little more enthusiastic when interviewing with the partners.

"What about the attorneys here? What do you think of them?"

She pursed her lips and exhaled loudly through her nose. I stared at her and just about managed not to smile.

"The attorneys here have all been hugely successful. It would be an honor to learn from them."

"You certainly learned a lot from me already. Do you remember what I taught you eight months ago?"

"Yes," she replied. "Never invite an arrogant asshole back to your apartment. It will only end in disappointment."

Now I laughed. I couldn't help it.

"The only disappointment was when you woke up the next morning and found me gone."

"You're right," she admitted. I raised an eyebrow, slightly surprised that she had given in so easily. I'd expected her to deny it; to fight against how much she wanted me. "I *was* disappointed. You stole my underwear."

Ah yes, the panties. They were still tucked away in a drawer in my apartment. There was nothing special about them, not to look at anyway. But the smell--oh

God, the smell of her sex had been addictive. Every day for a week after we'd fucked, I'd pulled those panties out of the drawer and smelled the crotch, hoping to draw out her scent for one more day. Finally the scent disappeared, and I was left with just a used pair of white cotton panties.

I still looked at them all the time. There was something mesmerizing about them. They contained memories of that night. I could still remember slipping them off her legs before I tasted the wetness between her thighs. The panties were all I had to remind me. Until now, that is.

I often took a pair of panties as a souvenir from women I'd fucked, although they usually just got thrown in a drawer and never saw the light of day again. That hadn't been the case with April's but I had no idea why. What was so special about her? The panties themselves were bland and boring, but she hadn't been. Definitely not. She was far kinkier than initial appearances had led me to believe. Perhaps she would even be up for a repeat performance right here on the desk? Perhaps not. She looked pretty pissed at me right now.

"You can have the panties back if you like," I said. "Just come back to my apartment. You might have to dig through my collection to find them though." That was a lie; they were right on top and had been for eight months.

"Just keep them," she muttered. "Are we done here?"

"No, Ms. Rhodes, we are not done here." I put my serious lawyer face back on. "What's your favorite position."

"Fuck you," she snapped.

Damn, this girl had a temper on her. I liked that.

"I meant, what position would you like to work at in the firm of course. M&A, corporate, tax, and employment law are our main areas of expertise. It was an honest enough question, Ms. Rhodes. You must have a really dirty mind."

"M&A," she replied, each syllable taking all her effort to speak aloud.

"Okay, I'll make a note of that. You will have to be flexible though. Are you flexible, Ms. Rhodes?"

"Yes, very."

"Good, good. I value a flexible lawyer. One minute I might want you doing one thing, and then the next I will want you to turn around completely and do something different."

"I'm happy with the lawyers here putting me in whatever position they like," April replied. "In fact, I've met a few today that I would very much like to get to know better."

Ouch. Who would she have met? Hopefully she was referring to Adam. He was the only guy who could even come close to me in raw sex appeal, but he was happily married and would never stray.

Was I jealous? I suppose I did like the idea of fucking her again. I'd certainly rather it be me making her come than someone else. It had been eight months since the last time so I didn't think that should count as going back for seconds. As long as we didn't do anything stupid like go on a date it should be fine.

"I'm afraid you'd be working with me a lot if you got the job," I said, sitting back in my chair and trying my best not to stare down at her tits. If I closed my eyes I could picture them, but I didn't want a mental image. I wanted to see them in the flesh. I wanted to suck on them again. To make her whimper, half in pain, half in pleasure when I took the nipples between my teeth and bit down hard.

"Aren't you a bit important to be working with a summer associate?" April asked.

"Yes, I like to think so, but I'm also a damn good lawyer. One of the best here, so they'll want you to learn from me."

"Sure you're not too busy doing managing partner things to keep an eye on me?"

"Managing partner things? I'm not the managing partner."

"But I thought… you're Foster Arrington right? The firm's name is Arrington & Hedges."

"Christ, how old do you think I am?"

No doubt having the name Arrington helped me get taken seriously in the early days, but I was a few years off being a partner and managing partner was a least a decade away.

"I just assumed… never mind."

"My mom is the managing partner," I explained. "And her dad was the founder of the firm."

"Oh."

I smiled, and took in the look of embarrassment on her face. She truly was stunning to look at. I'd seen her angry, embarrassed, horny, and upset. She was always beautiful.

"I take it things didn't work out at Cooper & Cooper?" I asked.

"No," she snapped, looking angry again now. "Of course not. Something to do with an associate getting punched and pushed down the stairs."

"Ah yes," I said, thinking back to the look on Zach's face when I'd decked him. Happy days. "That was fun. I never pushed him down the stairs though. I punched him and he fell."

"The distinction appears to have been lost on his dad, the managing partner of the firm."

"Oops. Be honest though, you don't regret me punching him do you."

April pouted, but she broke into a smile. A wonderful smile. "No, I suppose not."

"Good." An alarm notification popped up on my screen. I wanted to carry on this conversation all day, but duty called. "I have to go. Important meeting."

"Sure," April said, standing up. "There's not much point in this carrying on anyway. Obviously I can't work here with you."

"Don't trust yourself around me?" I joked.

"Think that if you want."

I let her storm out of the office, leaving another mental image of her ass in my mind. That girl could certainly pull off formal office wear.

She was right though, this wouldn't work. I couldn't let her spend the summer here. We might have a lot of fun working late and getting freaky in the office, but I didn't trust her not to fall for me. She might be mad at me now, but that would soon change and then I'd have to break her heart. I never enjoyed doing that, but it was a necessary evil for someone who looked as good as I did.

I emailed Mom and told her that April wouldn't be suitable. I knew I was potentially messing up her career as a lawyer before it had even begun, but I couldn't risk having a distraction like her around all summer.

The next few months were important. I had a couple of huge projects that demanded all my attention, and if April was sat just across the hall I would be constantly distracted.

I didn't trust her not to fall for me, but it wasn't just that. I didn't trust myself either.

And *that* thought truly terrified me.

Chapter Eight

FOSTER

"They'll be here any minute, Foster," Mom yelled from downstairs. "Put some clothes on. I don't want you to meet Pierce in just your underpants."

I swore under my breath, and got changed into a pair of jeans and a shirt. This was not how I liked spending my Saturdays. Usually by this point I would just be recovering from last night's drinking and sexual escapades, and getting ready to prepare for another night.

Not this weekend. At Mom's insistence, I'd come home to upstate New York on Friday night, in preparation for the visit of Mom's new boyfriend for lunch on Saturday.

Mom had been through a few boyfriends since Dad died, but this was the first one she'd introduced me to. It must be serious. She'd already given me the whole spiel about him not replacing Dad, and that even though she loved this new man, she still loved Dad, blah, blah, blah.

I didn't care about any of that. What I cared about was Mom getting screwed over, and that's almost certainly what was happening here.

Mom hadn't told me a lot about Pierce, but what she had told me I didn't like. He had a job, but not a good one and by the sounds of it he barely earned enough to support himself and his daughter who was at college.

No doubt after a few months, Mom would start sending him money and paying for vacations. Before you knew it, he would have moved in and be living it up while she worked her ass off running a prestigious law firm. She had a hard enough time of it trying to manage the D.C. and New York offices. She didn't need a lazy bum scrounging off her as well.

I strolled downstairs and gave Mom some help setting the table for lunch. Mom had never been a traditional housewife. While Dad had been alive, the most she'd ever cooked was pasta with a sauce straight from a jar. And she'd burned that.

"The food smells good," I remarked, as the scent of a spicy sauce wafted in from the kitchen. "You have someone deliver?"

"No," she snapped. "I cooked it if you must know."

"Oh."

"You don't need to sound so concerned. I've been practicing."

"Why?"

"Because Pierce enjoys cooking. We do it together."

I carried on putting out the cutlery as a cheesy image of Mom and this Pierce guy cooking together came into my mind. They probably flicked sauce at each other and all that soppy stuff.

"You've only set three places," Mom remarked when I'd finished putting everything out. Or thought I'd finished anyway.

"There's only three of us eating. Or do you have two boyfriends coming over."

"No, I only date one person at a time," she replied. "Unlike some people I know." She gave me a playful slap on the back of the head. She hated that I was a player and often scolded me for what she considered "unprofessional behavior." It's not like I was doing it with clients. Not recently anyway.

"To be fair, Mom, I don't *date* multiple women, we just--"

"I'm happy not knowing, son. Anyway, set another place at the table, please."

"Who for?"

"Pierce is bringing his daughter along as well."

"Oh great," I moaned. "I thought she was away at college."

"Me too, but she's come back for the weekend to support her father and to meet us. And she's not at college--she's at law school, so you two will have something in common."

I gripped the fork in my hand hard enough to bend the silver. Law students: I'd had more than enough of them while I was at law school.

"You know the one thing I hate more than lawyers?" I said. "Law students."

"I'm sure she's lovely. Just play nice and try to get through lunch."

Mom kissed me on the cheek and smiled, but when the doorbell rang she instantly started fretting and checking herself out in the mirror.

"I'll get the door, shall I?" I joked. It felt so weird watching my mom panic like she was on a first date.

I opened the door and came eye-to-eye with the man who had got my mother so worked up. He wore similar clothes to me, except his entire outfit looked like it cost less than my belt.

"Hi, you must be Foster," the man said holding out his hand. "I'm Pierce. Pierce Rhodes."

"Hi, Pierce," I said shaking his hand. The man had a decent handshake at least.

Wait, what did he say his last name was? Pierce *Rhodes. Rhodes.* Surely not. That wasn't possible.

"Well don't just stand there," Mom said, appearing behind me. "Let him in. Where's April?"

"She's just coming," Pierce said, turning to look at the girl walking up the path to our house.

April. April Rhodes. Oh shit. Oh fucking shit.

"You," I said, as she looked up, seeing me standing in the doorway for the first time.

"What are you… I don't…"

"Surprise," Mom exclaimed. "I said the two of you had something in common. But no talking about work today. Come on, let's eat, I'm starving."

"Come in, April," I said cheerfully, forcing a smile even though I still hadn't processed all this. "I must admit I have quite the appetite as well now. I'm desperate to get my lips around something sweet and tasty."

-*-

I quickly ruled out a paranoid theory that April had known about this all along. Pierce and Mom had been dating for a year, but they hadn't 'come out' until six months ago. Neither of us could have known when we'd slept together.

Judging by the look of surprise on April's face, she'd found out at the same time I had. She didn't look at all pleased by the news either, but she did her best to appear polite and keep up the conversation like a good little girl.

Pierce had obviously made Mom offer April the interview at the firm, which was why she'd turned up at my office at such short notice. Clearly this man had power over Mom. I didn't like that one bit.

"How's the food?" Mom asked.

"Delicious, Kathleen," Pierce said.

"Lovely, thank you, Mrs. Arrington," April said politely.

"Yes, it's great Mom. I haven't eaten anything so delicious in… oh about eight months."

April narrowed her eye and glared at me, but everyone else kept eating. I smiled and, when our parents weren't looking, I stuck my tongue out at her and slowly moved it up and down just as I had when my head had been between her legs. She looked down at her plate, but I caught a slight shiver run through her body.

April wanted me. That was natural enough. What did that prove? She wasn't blind. The weird bit was, I wanted her as well.

"How did the interview go?" Mom asked, although I couldn't tell who she was directly the question to.

"I sent you my comments in an email," I replied.

"Ah yes, I remember."

"Thank you for giving me the opportunity to interview," April said. "But I understand why I didn't get the job."

"Never mind," I said. "You'll find something. I'm sure a girl with your talents will find a position somewhere. Not everyone can be as good a lawyer as me."

"Foster, don't be so rude," Mom scolded.

"That's okay," April said. "Some people are just better suited to recording their time in six minute increments, aren't they Foster?"

"Hey, if six minutes is all I need to accomplish my goals then so be it. The client never complains."

"I bet you don't get many *clients* coming back for repeat work though," April said.

"April," Pierce exclaimed. "Now you're being rude."

"Sorry," April said sheepishly.

I grinned. She had a temper on her this one. All polite and 'daddy's little girl' one minute and then cheeky and rude the next. I liked it.

"We would love to have you at the firm," Mom said. "In fact, you should find an acceptance letter at your apartment when you get home."

"I will?"

"She will?"

April and I spoke in shocked unison.

"Yes," Mom said. "Everyone she interviewed with gave a rave review?"

"*Everyone?*" I asked, raising an eyebrow. "Are you sure?"

"Positive," Mom said, not looking me in the eye.

"Thank you, Mrs. Arrington."

"You really must call me Kathleen, dear. We're going to be family soon, after all."

"What?" I asked, my fork screeching to a halt in front of my mouth.

Mom cringed and shared a look with Pierce who just laughed and rolled his eyes. "So much for the big official announcement," Pierce said.

"Sorry," Mom said. "It just slipped out."

Pierce placed his hand on Mom's, and looked up and April and me. "We were going to save the news for after lunch, but apparently lawyers aren't as good at keeping secrets as I had assumed."

He looked over at Mom and smiled. She looked embarrassed, like a kid who'd been caught kissing her boyfriend by her parents. It would be cute if I didn't know exactly where this conversation was going.

"Pierce and I are getting married," Mom said excitedly. "Any chance you're both happy for us?"

April reacted before I did. "Of course. Congratulations." Mom and April shared an awkward hug.

"You got your feet under the table pretty quick, didn't you," I said to Pierce. "Here was me thinking you'd wait a few more months before you started mooching off Mom."

"Foster!" Mom exclaimed.

"It's okay," Pierce said, remaining calm. "Foster, I'm not here to--"

"Save it," I snapped. "Mom, you're an adult, you can do what you want. Just don't expect my fucking support while you give away everything you've worked so hard for. Enjoy your dessert."

I stormed out without looking back at April. It was too soon for Mom to get married. She'd only known Pierce for a year. She'd dated Dad for five years before they got engaged. What was the rush?

And to top it all off, I would no doubt have to babysit April all summer at work. I wanted to fuck her, not hand her assignments. If I was going to punish her, I wanted it to be with a firm hand to her ass, not a load of redlines on a memo. I wanted to spend the night inside her, not pouring over client files together.

Well, I couldn't stop Mom getting married, but I could damn sure stop April having a good time this summer. I had too much money riding on these next few months. My clients were far more important than some piece of ass—however tasty—that I'd already fucked once anyway.

Oh, and she would soon be my stepsister.

April would be begging for the summer to end by the time I'd finished with her.

Chapter Nine

APRIL

It was only my second day and I was already begging for the summer to end.

The first day was one long introduction to the firm in the morning, followed by an afternoon of "Legal Ethics" which could have been boiled down to five minutes instead of three hours. Essentially, it was just 'don't betray client confidences.' Hardly rocket science, but at least I didn't have to see Foster.

Foster. My soon-to-be stepbrother, and existing pain in my ass. That mistake eight months ago had been much worse than I'd first realized. Meeting him again had a few advantages though. I'd been idolizing him. In my mind, he'd been not just a great shag, but a knight in shining armor. He'd come to my rescue and saved me from Zach. After that night, I'd put him on a pedestal, but he wasn't worth it. I knew that now.

Foster had acted like a complete prick when he'd interviewed me, but I could handle that. I was far more concerned with the way he had spoken to my dad. Dad hadn't deserved that. To be fair, I gave Dad an earful in the car on the way home, but that was different. I was his daughter.

I'd written off all hope of getting the job until Dad introduced me to his girlfriend--Kathleen Arrington. I didn't know what Foster had said about me to the other partners, but you didn't need to be a genius to guess the gist of it. He didn't want me working here, but unfortunately for him, the other partners hadn't felt the same way.

I didn't want to work with Foster any more than he wanted to work with me, but I did want to work here, for this firm. Arrington & Hedges had one of the biggest offices in D.C., and they were famous nationwide. They even had some international satellite offices to work with on global deals. Me being here was huge. I wasn't about to let Foster screw me over.

Speak of the devil.

"Come to my office," Foster said, standing in my doorway holding a cup of coffee.

He looked tired. Probably a late night of partying ending with... I didn't even want to think about how his nights ended. I knew what he liked to do after a few drinks.

"I have to do this conflict of interest list first," I replied, trying to sound polite. Other attorneys were still walking in and I didn't want them to think I was rude. With any luck, I could get assignments from them and not have to work for Foster at all. "I need to list all the clients I worked on last summer to make sure I don't create a conflict of interest."

"I know what a conflict of interest list is," he replied grumpily. "Come to my office when you're done."

I'd only worked on a handful of projects at Cooper & Cooper so my list of previous clients was a rather modest seven, and most of them I had only worked on briefly. I could only drag the work out for so long before I had to pick up a pen and a pad of paper and head to Foster's office.

The clock on the wall said 10:15. No one left the office before seven. This was going to be a long summer.

As usual, Foster had his door shut, so I knocked loudly and waited for him to let me in. I heard a grunt from the other side, so I opened the door and peaked in.

"Is now a good time?"

He waved a hand towards the chair, but didn't look up at me. Evidently his monitor held something far more interesting than me.

"Why didn't you come and see me yesterday?"

Asshole. "Morning Foster. I'm fine thank you. How are you?"

"I emailed you and told you to come by. I believe I said it was urgent. When a lawyer asks you to come by urgently you do it."

"They only gave me login details this morning and I haven't had time to check my email."

"Oh."

Ha. Serves you right for being an asshole.

"Apology accepted. Whose bed did you get out the wrong side of this morning?"

"Wouldn't you like to know?"

"Not really, no," I replied. I liked to think the day after we'd slept together, he'd at least gone to work with a smile on his face. He'd certainly had one while we'd been in bed together. I remembered him grinning at me as he came up from between my legs, and kissed me with lips that tasted like my sex.

Oh God, April. This is not the place for these thoughts. I crossed my legs, and tried to focus on what an asshole he was being so as not to leave a damp patch on his chair.

How could I be attracted to this jerk? He hadn't made any effort to apologize for the way he'd spoken to Dad at the weekend. He clearly didn't like the idea of his mom getting remarried, but he didn't need to take it out on me and Dad.

Foster finished working and turned his full attention to me. I almost shriveled up under his gaze, as I backed up into the chair, and wished I could turn invisible. Was that hatred in his eyes? Contempt? Or maybe he was just undressing me with his eyes?

"You look nervous," he said, tilting his head slightly to the side.

"I am a bit," I admitted.

"I didn't take you for the nervous type. You weren't at all nervous when I was between your legs."

"You can't talk about that anymore," I pleaded.

"What was it you said when I had my tongue in your pussy? 'Hurry up and fuck me.' That was it."

Yes. That was it. I could still hear myself saying those words. I wasn't the type of girl to speak like that. Even at the time, it was like the words had come from someone else. Like my body had been possessed. I suppose it had in a way. Foster had me completely under his control. He could have done whatever he wanted with me and I would have gone along with it.

"This isn't appropriate," I said meekly.

"Why? Because I'm your boss now?"

"Yes. And because you're going to be my stepbrother soon. Or had you forgotten that part?"

"No," he snarled. "I've not forgotten. I'm just not convinced it's going to happen."

"Why not?"

"I have a feeling that when I tell daddy what I've done to his little princess he's going to run a mile."

"You wouldn't dare." He wouldn't. Would he? He clearly didn't want his mother to get remarried but would he really act like such an ass? Who was I kidding--of course he would.

"Don't count on it."

I stared at him, trying to read the expression in his eyes, but instead I just lost myself in his gaze. I looked

70

down at my pad of paper, and scribbled the date at the top, just so I had something to do.

I could just about make out the bottom of one of his tattoos on his wrist where the shirt had ridden up slightly. Looking at him here in his office, no one would guess that his upper body was covered in tattoos. That part of my mental image was fading. When I pictured Foster at night--something I did far too often--the dark lines of the tattoos all sort of blurred into one, moving out of focus whenever I tried to concentrate on one particular part.

"Did you call me in here for something?" I asked when I couldn't handle him looking at me any longer. "Or did you just want to make inappropriate comments about a night I'd rather forget."

"I need your help on a case. You heard of PorTupe?"

I nodded. "Of course. They're a huge pharmaceutical company based in Delaware."

"Correct. We do a lot of work for the board of directors. Corporate compliance stuff. It's my biggest client by a long way. The board members have been named as defendants in a shareholder litigation suit. You know what that is?"

"It's when the shareholders sue the board for mismanagement," I guessed.

"Not always, but in this case that's pretty much it."

"How can I help?" I asked eagerly. The work probably sounded boring to ninety-nine percent of the population--hell, it probably sounded boring to ninety-nine percent of lawyers--but it was exactly what I wanted to do. Mom had done work like this, and I wanted to carry on her legacy.

"You get the enviable task of going through all the emails and flagging the ones that are appropriate to the litigation. You also need to mark any that are covered by attorney-client privilege."

"Doc review," I said, naming the project despised by all junior attorneys.

"Correct again," Foster said with a smile. "It's a shitty job, but someone has to do it. You'll get loads of billable hours out of it though. Go talk to Marvin to get more details about the project. He'll also show you how to use the appropriate software."

"Thanks." I had to expect this kind of work as a summer associate, but that didn't mean I had to enjoy it.

"This is time-sensitive as well. Looks like we'll be spending many more nights together. Feel free to come by my office if you get bored. I'm sure I can think of a way to make your time here more satisfying."

"I'm more than capable of taking care of that myself," I replied. "I haven't needed you for the last eight months, and I don't need you now.

"You still think about it, don't you?"

"No," I lied. "Never."

"I'm not against the idea of a rematch," Foster said, as if he was doing me a favor. "Sometimes after a long day of work I don't have the energy to pick up anyone new. You'll do as a bit of fun."

"Well with an offer like that..." I walked out of the office and shut the door.

We couldn't keep having that conversation. It was hard enough looking at him and not thinking about that night. It was next to impossible when he kept bringing it up.

How had those lips brought me so much pleasure when they were now causing me so much grief? I shouldn't even listen to him, but he was a hard man to ignore. He had... talents, I had to give him that much. But he was a prick.

And what a prick. Seven inches long, nice and thick, and fucking gorgeous to behold.

I turned my mind to the doc review project Foster had just given me, hoping it would act as a cold shower. It did, but as I'd discovered a lot over the last eight months, a cold shower was not enough to quench my desire for Foster.

I couldn't give in to him; he was my boss *and* my stepbrother--nearly--so he was completely off-bounds. That just made it worse. There was nothing like forbidden fruit.

I'd had eight dry months. Eight months without a man. How much longer could I last? I was only human, and Foster was... Foster was impossible to resist.

Chapter Ten

APRIL

After my first week of work, I needed a lot more than just a cup of coffee, but that was all I could convince Bryan to join me for. Unlike me, he actually had a loving partner who looked forward to seeing him at home. The closest I had to anyone who enjoyed seeing me was Foster, but that was just because he enjoyed torturing me.

I'd stayed late every night this week except Monday, and on two of the days I had been there past midnight. At least I didn't have to work at the weekend though. Not *this* weekend anyway.

I'd taken full advantage of the free meals the firm provided for employees working past seven, but when combined with the lack of exercise, I was a little worried about my figure. I had a naturally slim physique, but beyond a certain point I put on weight like anyone else.

How did Foster stay in such good shape? He must go to a gym nearby, but he seemed to be in the office more than me, so I had no idea where he found the time.

"Sorry I couldn't get you a government job," Bryan said as we sat down outside. D.C. tended to be dead after work on Fridays. Most people were heading out of the city, or popping home to get changed before a night out. Very few people in government jobs worked late on Fridays, or any night of the week for that matter, so the coffee shop near Bryan was almost deserted.

I didn't like sitting in the heat, but I'd been in an air conditioned office most of the week and this was a rare opportunity to breathe fresh air. Well, not *fresh* as such, but at least I was outdoors.

"Don't worry about it," I said. "Everything worked out in the end. Sort of."

"Sort of? Didn't you land your dream job?"

"I guess. I'm grateful, obviously, but--"

"But the work isn't an exciting as you'd hoped?"

"Doc review," I said, knowing those two words would say all that needed to be said.

"Ah. Yeah, I hear that's bad. Fortunately I don't need to do much of that for the DOJ. Not that it's all that exciting where I am either. Just lots of memos for the most part."

"I would kill for a legal memo to sink my teeth into," I said, only slightly exaggerating. "Anything that involves writing and legal analysis, instead of reading emails and clicking a button."

"That's weird," Bryan said, setting his coffee down on the table. "Don't all the big firms outsource doc review these days? I thought it was all done on the cheap by lawyers in less expensive parts of the country."

"Yeah, I never had to do any at Cooper & Cooper. I guess Arrington & Hedges doesn't do…"

Foster. God damnit, he had given me a project that I shouldn't even have had.

"What's wrong?" Bryan asked.

"Nothing," I said. "Nothing at all."

"How are the people there?" he asked. "If you get on with your colleagues then you'll probably find time will go much quicker."

"Most of them are fine."

"Most?"

I sighed loudly, letting out some of the tension as I did so. Bryan gave me a weird look, but didn't say anything.

"My boss is my stepbrother," I said. "And he's an ass."

"I didn't even know you had a stepbrother."

"Technically, I don't. Not yet, but I will soon."

I told Bryan about my Dad's engagement to Kathleen Arrington. They hadn't talked much about wedding preparations, but Kathleen seemed like the type who would want a big wedding. At least that would delay the inevitable for a bit. But one day soon it would happen; Foster would be my stepbrother.

The stepbrother I'd fucked.

"What's so bad about this guy?" Bryan asked. "I'd have thought he'd be nice to you if you're going to be his sister."

"That's because you're assuming he's a mature adult. He's not. He's a cocky, arrogant, immature jackass. He does my freaking head in, but I can't avoid him. He calls me into his office every day."

"His name's Foster Arrington?" Bryan asked, looking at his phone. He must have found Foster's profile on the firm's website.

"Yeah, that's the one."

"He has good reason to be confident. That's one good looking guy. I'm as straight as they come, but even from this profile picture I can tell he's a catch. Look how wide his shoulders are."

"He's not my type," I said, refusing to look at the photo Bryan was showing me. Foster really wasn't my type. Not if you judge my type by the kinds of boyfriends I'd had in the past. None of them had been anything like Foster.

But I suppose if you judged 'type' by the kind of man that had you wet between the legs just by smiling at you--or not even that--then Foster was definitely my type.

"If you say so," Bryan said, giving me a knowing look. Could he tell? I felt like my face was giving away everything I'd done with Foster, but that was probably just paranoia.

"Even if he is good looking, and I still insist that he's average at best, he's a complete prick. You should hear the way he talks to me."

"What sort of things does he say?"

So many things. Every night this week he'd called me into his office once most people had left and he always said something inappropriate. That we should fuck again to pass the time. That I should bend over his desk while he decides what to do with my ass. That he's hungry for something sweet and wants to go down on me. That I talk back too much and need something to fill my mouth.

"He's just mean," I said pathetically.

"You might have to get used to that. Lawyers talk that way, it's just part of the job."

"I suppose. It just hurts coming from him, that's all."

Bryan raised an eyebrow. "Are you sure you don't like him?"

"Ew, gross. He's going to be my stepbrother. I meant it's a shame he couldn't be nicer for the sake of being a happy family and all that."

"Okay," Bryan said, raising his hands in defeat. "If you say so."

Damn it, was I that transparent? What if other people at work were picking up on it? That wasn't likely. The other attorneys were far too consumed with billing as many hours as possible to notice any kind of sexual tension. If that's what it was.

I still thought he was a genuine ass because of the way he'd acted with Dad and me, but he had a good side too.

Foster had been a cocky shit that night eight months ago, but there had been more to him than that. He been protective, supportive, and kind. Which was the real Foster and which was the act?

I'd find out soon enough. I just hoped I didn't get hurt in the process.

Chapter Eleven

FOSTER

I couldn't keep this up much longer.

Giving April that large doc review project to work on kept her in the office until late at night, and gave me plenty of excuses to call her into my office for some one-on-one time, but sooner or later I would have to outsource the work to someone cheaper.

Usually a fifth-year associate wouldn't get near client billing, but being the son of the managing partner did have some advantages. I wrote off most of April's time. There was nothing wrong with the quality of her work, and she got more efficient with each passing day, but my clients wouldn't pay $400 per hour for a summer associate to do doc review when they knew we could outsource it for less than half the price.

April craved a real assignment, something she could get her teeth stuck into, but I hated passing on work to inexperienced attorneys. My clients expected the best and, when I did the work myself, I knew that was what they got. If I let junior associates help, then mistakes would slip in.

The classic error was quoting case law out of context. New attorneys like nothing more than finding a juicy quote in a case and then sticking it in a memo to nail the point they were trying to make. Unfortunately, they often didn't bother to check whether the quote had any actual relevance to the facts at hand.

I'd once let that slip by me, but opposing counsel spotted it and their reply brief tore me a new one. Now I checked and double checked everything until I trusted the other attorney completely.

How much could I trust April? I saw hatred in her eyes when she looked at me. I shouldn't have acted like such a dick towards her father, but he deserved it for trying to mooch off my mother.

However, as much as April hated me, she loved being a lawyer, or at least the idea of being a lawyer. Over the last week, she'd made the odd comment here and there which made it clear she was trying to follow in her mother's footsteps and become a hotshot corporate lawyer.

Not many kids dreamed of becoming a corporate lawyer, but given that I had also followed in my mom's choice of career, I probably shouldn't be too quick to criticize. I didn't do it to keep Mom happy though.

I was a lawyer to make money. Corporate law paid well, and being a fucking awesome corporate lawyer paid fucking awesomely well. When clients bypassed the designated partner and went straight to the associate you knew you were doing something right, and that had been happening with me for years.

Even if Mom hadn't been managing partner, I'd still have gotten every pay raise I'd requested. The official lockstep pay scheme had long ago been broken with my salary and there were even a few partners who looked enviously at my pay. Served them right for being shit at rainmaking. The money was there for those who knew how to earn it, and I was definitely one of them.

As much as I would love to discipline April, I had something a lot sexier in mind than tearing her apart for not being a good lawyer. What work could I give April that she wouldn't completely fuck up? I had a couple of projects in my inbox that could be delegated, but I had no real idea what April's skill set was.

I found her official application on the computer system and browsed through her resume. Career offices at law firms insisted on making all students use a certain template for their resume, so I could always tell what school someone went to just based on the outline of their resume. It made reading the things even more boring that it was already, however April's did reveal a lot about her.

April's undergraduate GPA was stellar; easily good enough for her to have gone to one of the holy trifecta of Yale, Harvard, or Stanford law schools. Unless she'd completely fucked up the Law School Admission Test, she would have been accepted at a much better law school than the one she now attended.

The reason she chose her school was on the next line down. April had been granted a full-scholarship to cover the entire cost of tuition. No doubt that had been almost impossible to resist for someone whose family struggled financially. Going to Harvard would have been great, but it would have come with a debt that she'd have been paying of for decades.

Her grades at law school put her in the top five percent, so she would likely graduate with top class honors. Unfortunately, law school grades were a poor predictor of a student's ability as a lawyer.

I browsed through the writing sample she'd provided. It was an objective memo on some niche legal issue surrounding workplace discrimination. I didn't know much about that area, but I recognized good legal writing when I saw it.

The memo was supposed to be objective, but in a few places she'd let her bias slip through. I could tell that she'd come to a conclusion first and then tried to fit the argument together to arrive at that conclusion. That didn't mean the memo was inaccurate, but it would have been stronger if she'd remained more objective. Still, it was a common mistake by law students.

April could handle this task. Besides, I owed her one. She'd lost her last job because I had been unable to resist punching that smarmy jackass who'd tried it on with her. I didn't regret it. I only punched people who deserved it, and he had definitely deserved it.

I sent April an email summoning her to my office, and she appeared promptly a few minutes later. No doubt she welcomed the break from reading other people's emails.

"What can I do for you?" she asked professionally.

Today she wore a light cardigan over her blouse which further obstructed my view of her breasts. It had been nearly nine months now since I'd had those nipples in between my teeth, and I desperately needed another look.

"You cold?" I asked.

"I find it's always a little chilly in your office," she replied. "You have the AC turned up too high."

"You know, if your nipples get stiff every time you come into my office, that's probably not because of the temperature."

April sighed and placed her pad of paper down on my desk. "Are we going to do this again?"

"Do you want to do it again? I'm game if you are. I have a meeting in ten minutes, but we both know that's more than enough time for me to send you back to your desk satisfied."

"If you say so," she mumbled in response.

I walked around the desk and sat on the chair next to hers. We often sat next to each other when going over her work. Most people were hot and sweaty by the time they made it to work--an unfortunate consequence of living in D.C.--but April always smelled like she was fresh from the shower. There was a hint of coconut today, but I'd also detected citrus and mint over the last week. The girl liked to mix up her shampoo.

"Did you call me in here for a reason?" she asked, looking straight forward at the now empty seat on the other side of the desk.

"Yes, I have something I'd like you to do for me."

"Okay, tell me about it."

"It's hard. Very hard. And big. I wouldn't give this to just anyone, but I know you can handle something hard and big."

"Your firm has a sexual harassment policy," she said stiffly. "Perhaps you should read it sometime."

"I believe the manual talks about 'unwelcome' contact. Is this unwelcome?"

I placed my hand on her thigh. She jumped at the contact, but she didn't tear my hand away.

"You can't do this," she gasped. "We work together."

"I do what I want," I replied. "And right now, I want to do you."

Finally, she turned to look at me. Her face had turned a light shade of red, but her eyes gave away her true feelings. She wasn't angry with me any more, even though she had every right to be. She wanted me. I could see it.

A quiet gasp escaped from her mouth as I removed my hand from her leg. "Soon," I whispered in her ear. "I'm going to have you soon."

I leapt up from my seat and went back to the other side of the desk, leaving April looking lost for words. "Now then, I have a new assignment for you."

April stared into the distance for a few seconds, then shook her head and snapped back into the zone.

She'd gone from looking desperate for my touch to the consummate professional in seconds.

"About time. I was wondering how much longer you'd be able to keep me on that assignment when you're supposed to be outsourcing it."

"You knew about that?"

"Of course. Despite what you may believe, I'm not actually stupid."

No, you're not. Definitely not. The only stupid person here was me. I'd drastically underestimated April, and I knew why. I was letting my desire to fuck her again cloud my judgment. That wasn't like me at all, but then neither was going back to a woman I'd already claimed. No one had ever enticed me back for seconds, but right now I couldn't think about fucking anyone other than April.

That was dangerous. Very dangerous.

Chapter Twelve

APRIL

I went back to my office after meeting Foster, but I couldn't concentrate on work. It was nearly lunchtime, so I decided to sneak out for a walk to try and clear my head.

I'd hoped that things would get easier the more time Foster and I spent working together, but they were just getting worse. He had a hold over me that I didn't understand. I hated him. When he spoke, I wanted to tear my ears off just so I wouldn't have to listen to his arrogant speeches about how it was only a matter of time before he would have me in bed again.

But every now and again, he would say something nice. He often praised my work, and thanked me for working long hours to get the project done.

Then there was the way he looked at me. He always had that hunger in his eyes. It had been there the first night we met. Every time I saw him, my mind flashed back to that night. The time he looked up at me from between my legs. The moment our eyes met as he fucked me while holding my knees up by my ears. That time in the middle of the night when we'd gone a little slower, his eyes only visible in the street lights that illuminated my room through the cheap blinds on my windows.

I had to use all my energy to stay mad at him, but when he touched me the chemical reaction in my body was impossible to resist. There was nothing I could do to stop the wetness appearing between my legs. I hadn't even been able to take his hands off me because my limbs didn't work. I'd felt paralyzed, completely unable to move. He could have had me right then and there and I wouldn't have been able to resist. I wouldn't have wanted to resist.

Yeah, I definitely needed a walk and some fresh air.

The temperature was due to exceed ninety degrees today, but there wasn't as much humidity in the air as usual. I wouldn't say the walk was pleasant, but at least I wouldn't need another shower.

Not many employees bothered to take advantage of the showers the building had on the ground floor, but I used them every morning. The shower in my apartment had the water pressure of a leaking tap, so these were a luxury I had to tear myself away from after ten minutes.

Going outside didn't help me get away from the lawyers. D.C. was full of them, and H Street in particular seemed to exclusively consist of lawyers and lobbyists, apart from a scattering of people working in the local coffee shops that served them.

It always struck me as odd that so many people would hold business meetings in coffee shops and talk so openly about their work when they had absolutely no privacy. In the five minutes I waited in line for my coffee, I heard enough about one deal to identify the buyer and I had a fair idea who the target was as well. Legal Ethics 101 should include a lesson on not holding important meetings in coffee shops.

Once I had my coffee, I strolled back to the office in a better mood than I had been in days. I only had one more afternoon of doc review, and then I could get stuck into the legal memo Foster had assigned me. I would still be working closely with Foster, but that couldn't be helped. I might even stay late tonight to get started on it.

With the help of a strong coffee and knowing the end was in sight, the doc review project flew by that afternoon, and if I kept going at the same pace I would finish the last batch of emails by four o'clock. I considered heading home early for the day, but that was always frowned upon at a place where most associates stayed until the sun had set.

The end was in sight when I came across an email that stopped me in my tracks.

Over the course of reading thousands of emails, I'd learned a lot about the inner workings of the company, including the fact that it had recently completed an investigation with the Department of Labor relating to diversity in recruitment.

The company had a decent mix of men and women, and all races were represented, but during a random inspection the DOL had discovered that the women and ethnic minorities were primarily placed in non-management roles.

At the end of the audit, the company--which essentially meant the three white male directors--had promised to improve its selection procedures and actively work to get more women and minorities in the top roles.

None of this was part of the case at hand, so I didn't have to flag any of those emails. I probably shouldn't even have been reading them, but I knew a bit about employment discrimination and found it interesting. Anything to get through the day really.

The email that caught my eye today was between the three directors. The email chain was one long conversation between the three men who sounded like they were still immature frat boys and not in charge of a multi-billion dollar company.

The way they talked about female employees was frankly disgusting, and their attitudes to anyone who wasn't white was even worse, but the parts that jumped out at me were the references to the DOL audit.

The email chain made it clear that the directors were actively falsifying the information going to the DOL to make the company look like it was hiring women and minorities in positions of influence.

The scam involved selective interviewing for positions that didn't exist. The company could say it had interview women and minorities, and chosen not to hire anyone. It looked better than always choosing the white male instead.

I might be just a law student, but I knew fraud when I saw it. The law firm might even be an unwitting accomplice in the company's reports to the DOL. I had to tell Foster.

His office door was closed, but then it always was. I walked over and was just about to knock when I heard a women giggling inside. It was Foster's paralegal, a cute young Asian girl who had a 'butter wouldn't melt' look about her. I stayed by the door for another second until I heard her laugh and say "I can't do that here."

At least if Foster had moved on to someone else, it meant we could now talk about work without him making a move on me every five minutes. That seemed like scant consolation next to the mental image of him screwing his paralegal on his desk. I knew he wouldn't have done that during the middle of the day--probably not, anyway--but I couldn't shake the look of her on her knees, taking him in her mouth while he sat at his desk writing me an email.

I'd never sucked him off that night, even though he had gone down on me plenty of times. Foster probably thought I was a selfish bitch who just let the man do all the work. I could've shown him that wasn't true, but it was too late. I'd played hard to get for too long. If I'd given in right away we could have kept it fun and casual. Now it would be a big deal, and my head couldn't take that kind of pressure.

I ran back to my desk, and emailed Foster requesting a few minutes of his precious time. The paralegal left his office ten minutes later, straightening her skirt as she walked out. A few minutes later Foster let me know he was available, so I headed over with the incriminating emails in hand.

"Yeah, come in," he said casually from inside his office. He sounded relaxed. Why would he be relaxed after having his paralegal in here? I tried not to think of that as I walked inside and sat down.

"What is it?" he asked.

Foster had one more shirt button open than usual, but he didn't look particularly disheveled. What did that mean? Had they just been flirting?

"I found something doing doc review."

"You've been doing it for a week. I should hope you've found quite a few somethings by now."

"Something bad," I explained.

Foster raised his eyebrows and relaxed back in his chair. My eyes flicked down to his crotch which was just visible over the edge of the table. His zipper wasn't undone. Another positive sign.

"Like what?"

"Do you know about the Department of Labor audit the company went through last year?"

Foster nodded. "I know about it."

"But we didn't help with it?"

"No, they handled that one with different counsel."

"Good."

"Why is it good that tens of thousands of dollars went to another law firm instead of mine?" Foster asked.

"Because the company is filing false audit reports with the DOL. Look at this email."

I handed Foster the email chain and gave him a few minutes to flick through it. I kept waiting for his face to change as it dawned on him how bad this was, but he remained emotionless the entire time.

"I agree, this doesn't look good," Foster said as he placed the emails down on his desk. "Fortunately this has nothing to do with the case, so we don't need to disclose these emails."

"I know that, but what are we going to do about it?"

Foster frowned. "Nothing of course."

"They're committing fraud," I said incredulously. "We can't keep working for them."

"We fucking well can," Foster replied. "Do you have any idea how much we bill them each year? They're my biggest client."

"They're discriminating against women and minorities, and then lying about it to the federal government. Do you want clients like that?"

"Yes," Foster replied casually. "Clients who do bad things often need lawyers to help them when they get caught doing bad things. If everyone in the world treated each other with respect and acted honestly all the time I'd be out of a job."

I simultaneously couldn't believe what I was hearing, but also believed that he did mean every word. Foster only cared about the money. I knew becoming a corporate lawyer wasn't exactly about defending liberty, but that didn't mean you had to turn a blind eye to things like this. My mom would never have stood by and let this happen.

"We have to tell someone," I pleaded.

"No, we certainly do not. We owe our clients a duty of confidentiality. That means you don't go ratting them out to the government. For fuck's sake, April, you need to learn to remain detached from the more unsavory side of this profession."

"You mean I should just ignore discrimination?"

"No, you can call it out, just not when you're being paid to defend a client."

"This is ridiculous."

"It's life. Get over it."

I growled. I couldn't help it. The noise sounded pathetic, like when Simba tried to pretend he was a grown-up lion in *The Lion King*.

Foster stared at me and then burst out laughing. "What on Earth was that?"

I laughed as well, and rubbed my face with my hands. I'd just growled at a senior attorney. Okay, so we'd done a lot worse, but I'd been the one insisting we act professional. I couldn't just growl when I didn't get my own way.

"Sorry, I don't know what came over me. That wasn't appropriate. I think I'm just tired."

"I don't mind you being inappropriate," Foster replied. "I encourage it in fact."

"Like you do with your paralegal?" I asked, the question slipping out of my mouth before my brain could stop it.

"Jealous?" Foster said, grinning that stupid, sexy grin of his.

"Only of her ass," I replied. "I'd kill for an ass like that."

"No, it's too small. I'm all for a slim figure, but I need something to sink my teeth into. Now, *your* ass is just right. Did I ever bite your ass that night?"

"No," I replied, suddenly feeling like I'd missed out on something special. "Not my ass."

"That's a shame. Well, maybe next time."

There won't be a next time. Those were the words that should have come straight out of my mouth the second he'd finished speaking. Instead I stayed silent.

There *would* be a next time. I knew that now. I didn't know when, but it was inevitable.

"You should go home," Foster said, breaking the silence. "You've been working late a lot, and I need you refreshed before you get started on that memo."

I nodded, and headed towards the door. I knew he was looking at my ass, but this time I didn't care.

"April?"

I turned around as my hand was on the door handle. "Yes?"

"My paralegal flirts with everyone in the office. You don't need to read anything into it."

"Okay." I shouldn't care. He could fuck whomever he wanted, and I'm sure most nights he did. I grabbed my purse, and headed out the door, not making any effort to hide that I was leaving early.

Foster had gotten in my head, and I didn't know how to get him out of there. I didn't know if I wanted to; I was enjoying the company.

Chapter Thirteen

FOSTER

April was undoubtedly a woman of many talents. Despite her timid demeanor, she'd been a live wire in bed that night nine months ago, and judging by this memo, the girl had some legal writing skills as well. There wasn't much sexier in life than a girl who was a good fuck, and could bill $400 an hour. Not for the same thing, of course.

April had earned a place in the meeting today, so I had my secretary send her an invitation. The whole point of the meeting was to discuss the findings of the memo, so who better to be there than the person who wrote the damn thing? Unfortunately, that meant introducing her to Jacob. He was an ass. A very rich and successful ass, but an ass nonetheless. He loved himself and thought he was God's gift to women.

We probably should have been best friends, but something about him rubbed me the wrong way. I never left these meetings in a good mood, and this one wasn't likely to be any different.

My secretary let me know Jacob was waiting in the large meeting room, so I swung by April's office to collect her. She'd been sitting there, waiting with her trusty pen and pad of paper, looking nervous as all hell. This must be her first client meeting. It would likely be a baptism of fire.

"You ready?" I asked.

"Yes," she said eagerly, standing up and following me down the hall.

"No need to be nervous," I said.

"Do you need me to do anything in particular?"

"Just introduce yourself, and present the findings of your memo and your legal conclusion. I need you to lead the meeting because I haven't read it."

I kept walking but noticed that April was no longer following. I turned around and saw her standing still, staring ahead, looking frightened. Frightened and beautiful.

"You haven't read the memo?" she asked nervously. "What if it's all wrong? I can't lead the meeting, I don't know--"

"Relax," I said, interrupting her as she spoke faster and faster, the panic audible in her voice. "I'm kidding. I've read the memo, and I'll lead the meeting. Just sit there and look pretty."

She breathed a sigh of relief, and resumed walking. "You're a complete bastard, you know that?"

"You wouldn't be the first woman to call me that," I admitted. "Come on, let's get this over with."

I opened the door and let April walk in front, although she didn't introduce herself to the client until after I had shaken his hand. Jacob appeared to be in one of his pleasant moods today. With any luck we would get through this meeting without him being a complete shit.

Just before the meeting started, the partner technically in charge of Jacob's business came in and insisted on staying. Alan hadn't done any actual legal work for the client in years, but he still got all the credit when things went right, while passing the blame onto me if the outcome was ever less than ideal. Typical partner, really.

There was a slightly awkward moment where Alan and April had to pretend they already knew each other, despite the fact that they clearly hadn't met before. April thought on her feet and greeted Alan the way a summer associate would treat a senior partner--friendly, but with respect.

"Here's my card," Jacob said, handing his business card to April.

"Thanks. I don't have any cards yet. I'm just a summer associate."

I cringed. So much for pretending April was an actual lawyer and not just a law student. It was my fault, I should have mentioned it before the meeting.

"Oh," Jacob replied, his mood immediately turning sour. "Well, I hope I'm not paying for this training experience."

"No, of course not," Alan said immediately. As always, he caved to the client's demands, no matter how unreasonable.

"Actually Alan," I said calmly, "we *are* billing for April's time here today. I asked her to be in the meeting because she wrote the memo we're here to discuss."

"You've dragged me all the way in here to discuss a memo written by a student?" Jacob asked.

"What Foster means," Alan said, "is that April provided some research assistance, but that he actually wrote the memo."

April fidgeted nervously in her seat, and her hand swept some loose strands of hair behind her ears. I didn't want her to hear this, but the worst thing I could do right now was ask her to leave.

"That's *not* what I meant," I insisted. "April wrote the memo, and it's a damn good one. I've reviewed it and

I made a few tweaks to the language, but she knows it better than I do. That's why she's here."

"I'm not being billed for her time," Jacob repeated. "Train people on your own dime."

"In that case, you don't get the memo and I suggest we call an end to this meeting."

April cleared her throat, and spoke quietly. "Perhaps I should leave. I don't want to cause any trouble."

"Yes, dear," Alan said. "Please leave us men to it."

April's face went from nervous to angry and I knew why. Alan was a sexist pig. That's why he wasn't allowed to interview new associates anymore. April opened her mouth to speak, but decided against it and stood up ready to leave.

"Sit down please, April," I said gently. "I would like you to stay."

"Foster, I want a word with you," Alan said sternly. "Outside. Now."

"No," I replied.

Alan looked at me incredulous. It wasn't the first time I'd fallen out with him, but it was the first time it had happened in front of a client. Mom would give me an earful for this later.

Jacob sat back with a smile on his face. He was loving all this.

Alan took a deep breath and composed himself enough to speak. "Jacob is my client, Foster, so I will decide--"

"Jacob," I said interrupting Alan. "Who would you rather have serving as your legal counsel? Would you like to deal with Alan, whose main area of expertise is the Securities Act of 1933, largely because he was alive when they wrote it, or would you rather deal with me? The person who's been providing you with sound legal advice for the last five years."

"I would delegate the work," Alan said meekly. "It's not like I'd try to do it myself."

"I'm the best lawyer in the firm, Jacob. You want to take the risk with whoever Alan can find to work with him?"

Jacob looked at Alan who already looked defeated. I didn't usually take pleasure from showing up an old man, but the guy should have retired years ago. My paralegal had been in my office a week ago telling me all about the things he said to her. It was fucking disgusting and hugely inappropriate for a law firm.

"Alright," Jacob conceded. "But I'm still not happy about being billed for a trainee."

"She charges a lot less than I do," I said.

"If I may," April said timidly, before clearing her throat again. "I could go through the memo with you, and then you could decide whether it's worth paying for."

"Interesting," Jacob said, eying up April with what I hoped was just curiosity. "Okay, that's fine with me."

"I can agree to that," I said. April knew the contents of that memo better than I knew the contours of her chest.

"Me too," Alan said, although by that point we had all forgotten he was there.

April looked at her copy of the memo, but I suspected she was just taking a few moments to compose herself before speaking. How could this be the same woman who had shouted at me to fuck her? She'd not been lost for words when we were in bed together, but outside of the bedroom she was often timid and shy.

Most women were the other way around. All mouth until I got them in the sack, and then they suddenly didn't know what to do. Or worse, they thought they knew what they were doing but didn't have a clue. I still had no idea how some girls got the idea that they should clamp on to my dick with their teeth instead of lips. I shivered, as I had an unfortunate flashback to the last girl I'd had to educate on proper blow job technique.

April didn't have what I would call 'blowjob lips' but I didn't doubt her abilities. She'd kissed me firmly, with a decent amount of tongue. Not too much, but she didn't hold it back either. She'd know how to suck dick, and if she didn't, I would be a patient teacher.

I looked down at my own copy of the memo to fight the eagerness growing in my pants. The last thing I needed was to get hard in front of the client. Knowing Jacob, he'd think it was because of him.

"You asked what needed to be included in the disclosure to shareholders," April began. Her voice shook slightly as she spoke, but that didn't matter as long as the words made sense. "However, the better question is whether you need to make the disclosure at all."

"That's not the question," Jacob said. "I *know* that I need to make the disclosure."

"I disagree," April replied. "There's an exception in the Delaware Corporate Code for this situation when one hundred percent of the directors vote in favor of the resolution."

"But not all the directors are voting in favor," Jacob said. "If you'd have read my emails, you'd know that one of the directors is abstaining. He's against the whole thing."

"I read the emails," April continued. "He's not going to be at the meeting and he's not voting by proxy. You don't need every director to vote in favor; you need every director present at the meeting to vote in favor."

Jacob stared at April for a few seconds and then broke out into a big grin. God, I wanted to smack him one sometimes.

"I think I'm going to like working with you," Jacob said. "Keep going."

April went through the rest of the memo, and answered Jacob's questions the few times he interrupted.

I might as well not have been there until the end when we discussed strategy and the next steps.

"Impressive, April," Jacob said as the meeting ended. "If you don't want to work here after you pass the bar exam give me a call. I'm sure I can find something for you to do in my office."

Ugh. He might as well have licked his lips, his desire for her was so obvious. Was I that creepy? April didn't seem to mind. She thanked him for the offer and shook his hand.

"I don't need to tell you how brilliant you were in there," I said to April as we sat down in my office for a post-meeting debrief. "You knocked it out of the park."

"Yeah, I know," April replied, letting a confident smile spread across her face. She'd earned it. "I think Jacob took a liking to me as well."

"Uh, yeah, I think he did."

"He's a good looking bloke."

"If you say so," I grumbled.

"It's a shame I can't date clients."

"Well you're not a lawyer yet and he's not technically... actually you're probably right. You shouldn't date him."

"Jealous?" April teased.

"You've sure come out of your shell," I joked, to avoid answering her question. "Am I going to regret letting you into that meeting?"

"You like it when I'm more confident," April replied. "Is there anything we should discuss?"

"No, I suppose not."

April smiled and stood up to leave. She'd be walking on air for the rest of the day. Not every client meeting would go that well, so I wanted her to savor this moment.

She stopped at the door and turned back to me. "Thank you," she said softly. "For what you said."

I nodded. "You're welcome. Oh, April?"

"Yeah?"

"You can't sleep with clients, but there's nothing in the ethics guidelines about sleeping with other lawyers. Don't forget that."

She smiled and walked out the door. What just happened? I'd gotten jealous. Worst of all, she'd spotted it. That wasn't how this was supposed to play out. Women got jealous after I'd fucked them, not the other way around.

This was uncharted territory. As a lawyer, I didn't like the unknown. I watched April as she chatted to Paul while making a cup of coffee. She had a glow about her. A freshness that no one else in this office ever had. Even Paul was smiling, and he never looked happy at work. That's what she did to people. That's what she did to me.

I was in trouble.

Chapter Fourteen

APRIL

I didn't get anything done for the rest of the morning. Endorphins had flooded my body during the meeting, and I found it impossible to concentrate on work. Maybe I would enjoy being a corporate lawyer after all.

The memo had been fun to write, but I'd expected Foster to make loads of changes. He'd barely touched it. There were a few minor edits where he'd toned down my overly confident language, and he'd picked up a rather embarrassing typo of the word 'public' with an unfortunate letter missing, but that was it.

Foster had boosted my confidence to no end. He knew how to do that. Nine months ago, he had transformed a nervous law student into a sexually confident woman for the night, and now he had helped me be a real lawyer.

I preferred it when he was a complete jackass; at least then I knew where I stood. I knew enough about office politics to know that he had risked a lot by speaking to Alan like that. Alan might be a dinosaur, better suited to another century, but he was a senior partner. Alan would no doubt mention the incident to Kathleen and then he would be in the shit.

I considered emailing Kathleen and explaining what had happened, but Foster would hit the roof if I stuck up for him like that. Besides, we were all trying to keep things professional, and if Kathleen weren't soon to be family there was no way I would have emailed her, so I shouldn't do so now.

Foster's attitude towards the PorTupe case still bugged the crap out me, though. After finishing off the last memo, I'd had some free time, so I'd dug through PorTupe's client files. I didn't have to look far before I found more evidence that the three directors running the company were complete shits.

A lot of the sexism was subtle, but it was there, even in the correspondence between the client and attorneys at the firm. Emails to male attorneys were professional and serious, whereas any email from a female attorney was quickly responded to with a request for confirmation from another attorney who just so happened to be male. That could just be because the male attorney in question was more senior, but given what I knew about this client already I was inclined to believe the worst.

Arrington & Hedges hadn't helped PorTupe with the Department of Labor matter, but we had handled many employment disputes. Allegations of harassment against the directors were rife, but it looked like all the cases ended up settling. Foster hadn't handled those issues, but he still turned a blind eye to them when I tried to convince him that the client wasn't one we wanted on our books.

Foster insisted that no client was perfect and we couldn't pick and choose. He was right, but that just made me more frustrated with the whole thing.

I shouldn't have been surprised by Foster's attitude. Large corporate law firms didn't exactly have glowing reputations as protectors of individual liberties and basic human rights. These expensive offices in D.C. weren't paid for with the fees from poor clients.

Unlike Foster, Mom hadn't been driven entirely by money. She'd done plenty of *pro bono* work, so even if she did collect her paychecks from large corporations, she at least canceled that out by making a positive contribution to the community. Couldn't I do the same?

I went back through all the introductory emails that had landed in my inbox on the first day, most of which were still unread, and went through them until I found what I was looking for. The firm had a *pro bono* program, and all employees were allowed to participate. The hours worked on *pro bono* cases even counted towards billable hours requirements, so I wouldn't have to do it all in my spare time. Perfect.

I requested a meeting with the partner in charge of the program, and looked at the type of projects the firm worked on. I didn't lack for choice, but I also didn't appear to be suitable for any of them. I couldn't help with tenant disputes, because my knowledge of real property law was appalling. I only got a B+ in that class and I would be perfectly happy never touching that subject again.

Defending people on death row certainly sounded exciting, but I knew nothing about criminal procedure other than what I'd seen on television. Unless one of the cops hadn't read the defendant his *Miranda* rights I was basically out of ideas.

Then I found it. The perfect program for me to help with. The notes clearly stated that no prior knowledge was required, and it was certainly something I was passionate about given my family history.

I could make a positive contribution to people's lives while I was at the firm. That might not cancel out the harm I was doing by ignoring a fraud happening right in front of my eyes, but it would help me sleep better at night.

_*_

"You want to help with elder law?" Simon asked. He was the partner in charge of the *pro bono* program, and he'd been delighted to see I was interested in being a part of it. By the sounds of it, far too many of the attorneys here were like Foster and ignored their *pro bono* responsibilities in favor of billing more hours and earning fees.

"Yes please," I said. "I've had two grandparents who ended up in nursing homes near the end of their lives. I know how vulnerable people can be at that stage of their lives, and I'd like to help."

"It's not one of the sexier areas of law," Simon said. "But it's important. You're right about these people being vulnerable. You wouldn't believe some of the things I've seen. Kids trying to steal from their parents when they get older is surprisingly common unfortunately."

"I believe you."

I'd seen it happen. When I used to visit my grandmother, I saw kids practically forcing their elderly parents to write checks for large amounts when they clearly didn't understand what was going on. It was disgusting.

"Unfortunately, elder law also requires a lot of court appearances. Nothing difficult from a civil procedure perspective, but it does require an attorney."

"A law student isn't enough?"

"No, I'm afraid not. I would still love for you to do this, but you would need to find an attorney to work with. One who wouldn't mind doing *pro bono* work instead of pushing through the latest M&A deal for our illustrious clientèle. Good luck with that."

Simon gave me a puzzled look as my mouth stretched into a smile that covered most of my face.

"Don't worry," I said. "I know an attorney who would love to help."

Chapter Fifteen

FOSTER

I'd never been so enthusiastic to review the work of a law student before. Usually any work prepared by a junior attorney went right to the bottom of the pile, to remain there untouched until the issue became urgent.

Projects from April got my immediate attention. The quicker I looked at her work and made my edits, the quicker I could call her back into my office a late-night review session. Those never went according to plan.

I imagined her coming into my office late in the evening, where we would chat and flirt, until she opened a button on her blouse and told me to stop talking and fuck her.

April had grown in confidence ever since the meeting with Jacob, but I still knew such an upfront demand was a long way off.

That didn't stop me from getting hard every time she walked into my office. My cock knew what it wanted, and no amount of sensible thinking on my part could convince it otherwise.

I'd stand a much better chance of getting her bent over my desk, if I could stop insulting her father, but every time we met, he would somehow end up in the conversation and I couldn't resist calling him out for chasing after Mom's money.

Even now, they were both off at some lodge for the week, and you didn't have to be a genius to guess who was paying for that.

Money-grubbing bastard.

None of this was April's fault, and I didn't directly blame her, but she clearly didn't like me talking shit about her father. She'd need to develop a thicker skin if she was to become an attorney. No one sugarcoated anything in this profession. If you fucked up, you paid the price. Fortunately, I never fucked up.

At least Mom's mini vacation meant she hadn't had the opportunity to lay into me for the way I'd treated Alan at the client meeting. I'd ignored all her calls until she finally sent an email tearing me a new one, but emails were easy to ignore, and that's exactly what I did.

I pinged April an email telling her to come to my office. She'd be along as soon as she'd gathered up her trusty pen and paper, so I used the minute of free time to scan my unread emails.

I didn't like what I saw.

The first was an invitation to a networking event at April's law school. The school wanted lawyers to show up and talk about their careers. I'd been to plenty of those before. It was just a bullshit excuse for law students to network with lawyers in the faint hope we might offer them a job after graduation.

I didn't have time for that shit right now, but the sponsor for this event was none other than Cooper & Cooper. They were sending a few partners along, together with a junior associate. No need to guess which one.

Could I really sit on a panel with Zach and treat him with respect? Probably not. But if April was going...

I opened her calendar and saw that she had blocked out a few hours for the event. I couldn't risk her bumping into Zach again without being there to keep an eye on things.

I replied to let the career counselor know I would be there to talk about M&A transactions for twenty minutes and answer a few questions. Not exactly my idea of an exciting evening, but what choice did I have?

The second email that caught my eye held even worse news.

April knocked on the door and walked straight into my office without waiting for me to respond.

"What the fuck is this?" I yelled, scanning an email from Simon about doing *pro bono* work at some old folk's home.

"Something the matter?" April asked, with a butter wouldn't melt expression on her face. She knew.

"Why do I have an email with information about doing *pro bono* work with old people? You know what *pro bono* means, right?"

"It means for the public good, I think?" April replied.

"It means it's a waste of my fucking time, that's what it means."

"I don't think that's the literal translation."

"Is this your doing?" I asked.

"I signed up for the *pro bono* program, yes. And I requested working on elder law because I believe it's an important and underserved area."

"That's lovely. I'm sure you'll get a medal for your efforts. But why the fuck am I getting emails about it?"

"Because I can't appear in court by myself and need to work with a licensed attorney."

"Again, why me?"

"Because I love spending time with you, and I think we make a great team."

"Oh."

111

Well that was a kick in the nuts. I'd been thinking much the same thing recently, but this was the first time she'd said anything to that effect.

I didn't want us to "make a great team." I wanted us to fuck. A lot. But I suppose being a great team meant April had recognized the chemistry between us. I'd picked up on it the first time she'd looked at me. I could always pick up on the signs. It stopped me wasting time chatting up the few women in this city who weren't interested in having me fuck their brains out.

"And also you're obsessed with money, and I think this will make a nice change," April added. "It's about time you realized the world doesn't revolve around you."

Way to knock the wind out of my sails, April.

"Sounds like you just want to spend more time with me," I teased. "If that's the case, all you had to do was say so. I've got a nice bottle of wine back home, and enough condoms to get us through the night. We don't need to spend time with old people. That's not exactly my idea of foreplay."

"I wasn't aware you knew what foreplay was?"

"Foreplay is when I spend so long kissing the insides of a woman's thighs that she screams and begs me to fuck her."

April pursed her lips to fight back a smile. She didn't get angry at my references to our night together any more. That had to be a good sign.

If I had to do some shitty *pro bono* project just to get back between her legs then so be it.

We spent some time going through the brief I'd redlined. April still took my criticism on board, but she now fought back on certain points, insisting that her sentence was grammatically correct, or that we should be citing a case against us because the opposition would find it easily enough anyway.

I'd created a monster.

As April left my office, I opened the blinds and watched her as she wandered over to get some coffee. She stopped by Paul's office on the way back and stood in the doorway for five minutes laughing and joking with him. Her back always straightened as she laughed, which pushed her breasts up into the air. I couldn't have been the only one in the office who'd noticed that.

I always relished the challenge of taking a woman off another man, or taking on the competition of another admirer, but this time it was different. I would rather no other men in the office spoke to her at all, as ridiculous as that sounded.

April didn't belong to me.

Not yet.

But soon that would all change. I could sense it in the way she was looking at me. Her attitude towards me was warming. It wouldn't be long now. I looked down at my cock, making itself known in my pants. I looked away from April before my dick exploded in my pants.

"Not long now," I said out loud to my penis. "Not long at all."

Chapter Sixteen

APRIL

"You know I'm only doing this to get in your pants?" Foster said, as he parked his BMW in front of the nursing home.

"I don't believe that for a second," I replied. "First, you know full well that this isn't going to get you into my pants. Second, I saw you reading up on elder law yesterday evening, so you're taking this seriously."

"I'm a lawyer. I take all my work seriously, even when the clients can't pay me. That doesn't mean I want to be here."

He was lying. Simon had told me that he'd offered Foster a chance to back out after finding out that Paul would like to do the work, but Foster insisted on going through with it. That heart of his did have some warm blood pumping through it after all.

I introduced myself to the receptionist, who then led us down the hall to Mrs. Andrews room for our meeting. Foster had insisted that I take the lead with the client, and this time he wasn't joking.

After Jacob, I didn't think Mrs. Andrews would prove all that intimidating. The important thing was not to give away how little I knew about issues surrounding elder law and wills and trusts.

"Remember," Foster said before we entered the room, "you need to get the client's confidence. Don't worry about giving them the answers right now. We can always do the research back at the office, or call in the expertise of another lawyer. God only knows we have enough of them at the firm."

"In other words, we just need to not sound stupid?"

"Exactly."

"In that case, let me do the talking." I smiled and walked inside before Foster could respond, leaving him standing there looking speechless. That didn't happen often. Would it have been completely inappropriate to take out my phone and snap a picture?

"Good morning, Mrs. Andrews," I said loudly. "My name is April. And this is Foster. We're your lawyers."

"Bloody hell, love," Mrs. Andrews responded in an English accent. "I'm old, not deaf."

Foster snickered behind me, while my face became a faint shade of pink.

"Sorry," I responded more quietly. *Way to go, April. What do they say about first impressions?* I'd even introduced myself as a lawyer before having graduated law school and passed the bar exam, so I'd offended the client and breached ethics rules in the space of ten seconds.

"That's alright. Take a seat, you two." Mrs. Andrews motioned to two old chairs against the wall, while she perched on the side of the bed. "I actually am a bit deaf, truth be told, but I have my hearing aid in so I can hear you loud and clear."

Foster had mentioned starting the meeting off with small talk, but I had no idea what to say to someone like Mrs. Andrews. What could I ask her?

"Do you have any exciting plans for today, Mrs. Andrews?" I asked, trying to effect a casual tone of voice, but instead coming off stuffy and formal.

"No, dear, not really. Just trying to not die."

Foster laughed, but I didn't turn to look at him. No doubt he was loving watching me mess this up.

Screw the small talk. "How can we help you today, Mrs. Andrews?"

"For starters, love, you can call me Doris. I can't be doing with any of that 'Mrs. Andrews' crap."

"Okay, Doris."

"I'd like your help preparing a will. As you might have noticed, I'm on my last legs and I want to make sure my money gets to my son. I might not look rich, but I have a few quid tucked away, and some shares that might be worth something now."

A will. That should be easy enough. You could buy do-it-yourself wills online, so a big law firm like Arrington & Hedges was bound to have some templates on their servers.

"No problem at all, Doris," I said confidently, opening up my pad of paper to a clean sheet. "We'll just need to get some basic information from you."

Doris gave me her full name, date of birth, and address, which I made sure to write down slowly to give myself time to think. What else did I need to know? Details about the son, obviously, and other living relatives. That should be about it.

"What about your son, Doris? Can you give me his information?"

"I can give you his date of birth, but not his name or current address."

"You can't give me his name?"

"No. This is the tricky bit, I'm afraid. You see, I had him adopted immediately after he was born. I've never met him. I never had any children after him, so he's my only offspring. Assuming he's still alive anyway."

"A will has to be very specific," I said, reciting about the only thing I did know about the law around wills. "If you're too vague then a court will hold the declaration invalid and the money will pass to your nearest relative through the intestacy laws."

"Someone read a book last night as well," Foster whispered in my ear.

"My closest relative is my sister," Doris said. "But I do not want her getting her hands on my money. That bitch has been nothing but a thorn in my side for the last seventy years."

I wrote "sister = bitch" on my pad, and then turned to look at Foster to see if he wanted to offer any assistance. He just smiled at, as he sat there with one ankle resting on his knee as if he didn't have a care in the world.

"What about the father?" I asked. "Is he still... with us? Perhaps that could help track down your son."

"The father?" Doris repeated softly. She looked around the room, but wouldn't look me in the eyes. "Yes, the father. Well, uh..."

Foster laughed, completely insensitive to the situation as usual, but he leaned forward and finally looked ready to help me out.

"Doris, you dirty girl," he joked. "You don't have a clue who the father is do you?"

"Foster," I yelled, turning to glare at him and slapping him hard on the arm. "You can't talk like that to a client."

"And you aren't supposed to slap your boss," he replied.

"It's okay, dear," Doris said, grinning like a schoolgirl with a crush. "He's right. I don't have a clue. Couldn't even narrow it down to single figures to be honest."

I stared at her wide-eyed in shock. She looked like such a sweet old lady. I couldn't think of her as a crazy young woman, partying the night away with loads of different men.

"It was the sixties, dear," Doris continued. "Crazy times. Drink, drugs, and dick, that was how I spent my evenings. Don't tell me you don't like to have the odd wild night every now and again?"

"I couldn't agree more, Doris," Foster said. "Unfortunately, young April here can be a little uptight sometimes. She does enjoy the odd wild night though, I can vouch for that."

"Oh my God," I mumbled, biting my pen and looking down at my pad of paper hoping it would offer some resolution to this conversation.

"I bet you can," Doris replied. "I'd have been all over you in my day. I was quite the looker, you know."

"I believe you," Foster agreed. "And that English accent? I bet you were beating them off with a stick."

"If I'd stuck to just beating them off, then I wouldn't be in this predicament," Doris replied.

I nearly choked on my pen. "Maybe we should get back to the topic at hand."

"Alright, love, but take a bit of advice from me. Don't be afraid to live a little. For example, if you have a sexy boss who could show you a good time perhaps you could let him."

"Did you pay her to say that?" I asked Foster.

He held his hands up and shook his head. "The lady speaks the truth, that's all."

I tried to remain serious, but when Doris winked at me, I couldn't help but break into a smile.

We did our best to get all the information we needed from Doris, including details on the adoption center used, but there was a long road ahead of us if we were going to track down Doris' son. I didn't even know if it was possible.

"You enjoyed that, didn't you?" I asked Foster as we got back in the car.

119

"I can't help it if I'm a likable guy," he responded. "Women of all ages love me. You should be able to understand that."

"Not really," I lied. "How did you have the balls to speak to her like that in the first place?"

"You just need to learn how to judge the client, that's all. Why do you think I sat back and let her speak at first? I don't joke around with every client like that, but Doris looked game for a laugh. Plus I saw she had a small calendar by the bed with shirtless men on it. Figured she wasn't really the shy type."

"Alright, Sherlock, I'm glad you had a good time."

"You had a good time as well. Don't try to deny it."

"Fine, it was fun," I admitted.

Too much fun.

What did it mean if someone like Doris could spot the chemistry between Foster and I so quickly? Who else had noticed? People in the office? Kathleen? Dad?

"I'm still not happy about losing all these billable hours," Foster said. "You completely set me up there."

"As per usual, you came out on top."

"That's not the point. Don't expect to get away with it. I'm going to make you pay for that one."

"How?"

"That would be telling, wouldn't it?"

Foster liked to tease. I knew that all too well from our night together. I crossed my legs in the passenger seat to try and quell the desire that always arose inside me when I thought back to that night.

Foster was the expert manipulator. I couldn't stop him even when I knew he was doing it. I wasn't sure I wanted to.

Chapter Seventeen

APRIL

"Does this coffee smell normal to you?" I asked Paul as we gathered in the kitchen area before starting work for the day.

"Yes, I think so," he replied, after smelling the cup of coffee I had just poured myself from the machine. "Why?"

"Nothing, I'm just a little paranoid at the moment." It'd been over a week now since Foster had threatened to get revenge against me for dragging him into *pro bono* work, but so far he hadn't done anything. Nothing I knew about.

"Paranoid about the coffee? Is someone trying to kill you, April? Because if so, I'll... keep my distance."

"Oh, thanks," I replied, playfully slapping him on the arm, and nearly making him spill his own cup of coffee in the process.

"It's nothing personal, but I have kids to look after. Anyway, how are things at work? You're a few weeks into it now. Learning anything?"

"Yes, a lot. Foster has been really helpful, actually."

"I must admit, I'm surprised you're spending so much time with him. Most junior associates are scared of him, and he hates working with subordinates. I guess he has a soft spot for you."

Nothing *soft* about it, knowing Foster. "We get on well enough I suppose."

By the time I'd turned on my computer, I already had a mountain of emails to wade through. Foster insisted on keeping me copied in on all correspondence relating to the cases I worked on. It made me feel like part of the team, but it also meant I had to keep up-to-date on everything and was expected to know what was going on.

There was also an email from Foster summoning me to his office. I grabbed my cardigan, but noticed that I was still hot from my shower. Usually I had cooled down by now. The answer to that conundrum came through in another email explaining that there had been a problem with the AC overnight and that the system had to be restarted. We'd all be sweating for most of the morning.

"Morning Foster," I said, strolling into his office. He had a new assignment for me, so that meant I wouldn't spend an hour in here listening to him telling me all the mistakes I made in my last memo. Thank heaven for small mercies.

I sat down and stared at the view across the desk. Instead of being insufferably cold, Foster's office was stuffy and warm, so he'd rolled up his sleeves and opened a few buttons on his shirt.

The tattoos on his forearms captivated me as I tried to remember the pattern they formed on the rest of his body. I could see little flicks of flame at the top of his chest, as if it were escaping from his shirt, but I quickly got distracted by the outline of his taut pecs, teasing me with their subtle appearance.

I picked up a file from his desk and used it to fan myself. All that did was waft hot air into my face.

"Why don't you get undressed?" Foster asked.

I raised my eyebrows. "Subtle, Foster. Real subtle."

"Alright, well you're going to at least have to open a few buttons."

He had a point. I looked him in the eyes, challenging him to look down at my chest, as I opened two buttons on my blouse. "Screw it," I added, before opening a third button. My bra would be on show now, but it had to be better than fainting.

Foster didn't look down at my chest, not while I was staring at him at least, but he was clearly loving every minute of this.

"What's this new assignment you have for me?" I asked.

"There's no new assignment. I just wanted you to come in here while the AC was broken. God, I love that view."

Foster leaned back in his chair and stared at my chest, making no effort to hide his admiration for what he saw. I couldn't deny feeling somewhat flattered. There were at least five women in the office who, in my opinion, had far better tits than me. Mine were pert, but of average size at best.

"Like what you see?" I asked.

"For now. I want to see a lot more though."

"Okay, well I can strip off right here if you like. Maybe I could get under your desk and give you a blow job. How about that?"

"Sarcasm is the lowest form of wit, you know?"

"Perving at my chest is hardly a sign of intelligence either. You're like an animal."

"Yeah," he admitted, smiling at me as he raised those dark green eyes up from my chest to look directly at me. "I've been called an animal before. Many times."

"And you take that as a compliment?"

"When it's moaned by a satisfied looking woman I do, yes. How would you describe me after that night?"

Insatiable. Strong. Orgasmic. Earth-shattering.

"A thief. You stole my panties, remember?"

"You really are obsessed with those panties. Well, tell you what, if you come back to my apartment tonight, you can take them home with you."

"No chance," I replied.

"Don't trust yourself alone with me?"

"We're alone now and I'm just fine."

"No you're not," he said, as he stood up and walked over to me. He perched on the edge of the desk right in front of me, with his legs either side of mine. "You're hot and flustered. You want me to take you."

"I'm hot because the AC's broken, you moron." I hadn't been that hot in my office; now I felt like I was on fire.

Foster leaned forward and placed a hand on each knee. I flinched back in my chair, but there was nowhere to move. I didn't push him away. I always froze up when he touched me, and I had an awful feeling that wasn't just because of nerves.

"I'm willing to bet that if I were to part your legs now, I'd see a wet patch on your panties. You've been looking at me with hunger in your eyes since the second you walked through that door."

"I skipped breakfast," I replied.

His hands applied pressure to my knees, but I resisted his attempt to part them. He was almost certainly right about what he'd find between my legs, but I wasn't about to give him that kind of pleasure.

"I'm getting tired of these games, April. I've done the decent thing and admitted that I would be happy to fuck you again. All you have to do is say yes, and you get another night of pleasure."

"I have plenty of toys that can help with that," I snapped. "And they don't steal my panties."

Foster's hand slid up the inside of my thigh as his mouth moved slowly towards me. "I've had a lot of time to think about what I'm going to do to you next time," he whispered in my ear.

My heart raced in my chest as the scent of his aftershave wafted up my nose.

"We can't do this," I said meekly.

"I'm going to make you do more of the work. I want you on your knees, April. I want you to open up that pretty little mouth of yours and slide it down my thick shaft."

"We work together. I'll lose my job."

"I'm going to wrap my hands around your head and fuck your mouth with my rock hard cock right up until the moment I'm about to come. Then I'm going to pull out and spray my load all over those perfect little titties. You're going to be a sticky mess."

"We're going to be related. This can't happen."

I'd lost the argument the moment I uttered those words. The excuses weren't enough, and saying we couldn't do it was as good as admitting I wanted to.

"It's going to happen, April. Soon."

The tips of his fingers were just an inch from my panties. I let myself slip forward slightly in my chair until my sex grazed against him.

Foster looked me in the eyes, his face close enough that I could feel his breath, and then smiled.

I closed my eyes waiting for a kiss that never came. Suddenly Foster stood up straight, teared his hands from my thighs, and moved back to his chair on the other side of the desk.

"See you tonight, April."

"No," I snapped back. "You won't. I... I have a date tonight."

"A date?"

He looked more confused than jealous. "Yes, a date. With a guy named Bryan." Bryan was coming to the networking event at the law school, and we would be hanging out together. That was kind of like a date, right?

"Well, I'm still confident I'll see you tonight."

Cocky asshole.

I stormed out of his office, completely forgetting to do up the buttons on my blouse until I'd made it back to my office.

He'd won me over. I hated myself for it. I hated the way it had happened, but it had. I was so completely screwed. Or I soon would be.

Chapter Eighteen

APRIL

"Thanks for coming, Bryan. I owe you a coffee."

"Don't worry about it," he replied. "I was considering coming along anyway. You never know, one day I might decide to leave my comfortable government job for a soul-crushing private gig and then these connections might come in use."

We were supposed to be networking before the panel discussion, but nearly everyone who'd showed up early was a fellow law student. Actual lawyers tended to be far too busy to show up to a networking event early and hang out with people who couldn't help them get new work.

The table at the front of the room had space for five attorneys. One of them was bound to be a partner from Cooper & Cooper, hopefully not Zach's dad, and the others would probably be a mixture of attorneys from different practice areas and with different levels of experience.

They were all here to talk about their careers, and explain how they got started in their jobs. All information was completely useless. The partners in their sixties had just strolled into jobs straight from law school when the market was completely different. The truth of the matter now was that most students didn't much care what work they did as long as they had a job.

Still, we all had to play the game. I would sit there and look riveted by the discussion and maybe even ask the odd pertinent question or two. When the talk was done, I would go and shake hands and collect business cards. Maybe one of those attorneys would offer me a job one day. Unlikely, but stranger things have happened. Like sleeping with someone and then finding out they were your boss. And stepbrother.

"I take it you aren't confident of getting a job offer from Arrington & Hedges at the end of the summer, then?" Bryan asked. "I thought you'd be focusing all your energies on impressing the partners there instead of trying to find a new job."

"Let's just say I have reason to believe Arrington & Hedges is not a long-term solution for me. Besides, after what happened at Cooper & Cooper, I'm not taking any chances."

"Fair enough."

I still hadn't told Bryan about my one-night stand with Foster. All Bryan knew was that Foster was making my life hell in the office, which was technically true.

"Looks like they're about to get started," Bryan said, motioning towards the table with his plastic glass of cheap wine.

The previously empty table now had four attorneys standing around, together with one familiar face.

"Zach," I said out loud.

"Who?" Bryan asked. "Do you know the Cooper & Cooper guys?"

"I know one of them," I replied. *I know him far better than I'd like to.*

The four lawyers took their seats leaving one empty space at the end. Zach made himself right at home with other lawyers, even though they were all partners and he was just a second-year associate. He'd be absolutely loving this right now. As if his ego needed the extra boost.

One of the career counselors asked everyone to take their seats, which happened surprisingly promptly. A respectful hush descended over the room. Why couldn't movie theaters be like this?

"We're one man down," the counselor said, "but I think we'll get started anyway. I'll ask the speakers to give a very brief introduction of themselves and then we can get into more detail later."

The lawyers took it in turns to give their names and the area of law they practiced in. I shivered the second Zach started talking, and not in a nerve-tingling, 'what the hell is happening to my body' kind of way. More like I felt spiders crawling over my skin.

Zach described himself as an M&A attorney at the firm, and emphasized his last name, no doubt hoping people would think he was a partner instead of a junior associate who'd been given the job because of his dad.

I don't think anyone in the audience was fooled. Zach couldn't have been any older than twenty-six and he barely looked that. He had a baby face that perhaps some people would describe as cute. I just wanted to punch it.

Even though Zach should have had less to say than everyone else, he insisted on speaking for the longest, and didn't stop until the fifth and final attorney showed up.

"Sorry I'm late everyone. Where were we."

Foster. What the hell was he doing here?

"Isn't that--" Bryan began.

"Yes," I interrupted. "That's Foster Arrington. Meet the man who's made my life at work a living hell."

And sent me home hot and horny on a daily basis. Meet the man who's responsible for me getting through enough batteries to power the entire law school for a week.

"Hello everyone," Foster said confidently, not letting Zach resume speaking. "I'm Foster Arrington."

The atmosphere in the room changed in an instant. All the women were now either sitting in stunned silence, barely breathing, or gossiping to the person next to them like schoolgirls who'd just seen their favorite pop star.

As usual, Foster had the attention of the entire room. Me included.

-*-

Foster talked more than anyone else and most of the questions from the audience were directed at him. He named dropped a few of his major clients, including PorTupe and Jacob's company, and that captured the attention of the group.

"He's impressive," Bryan remarked after the panel. "Foster, I mean. The others were boring as hell, and don't even get me started on that smug little bastard from Cooper & Cooper."

"Zach. Yeah, he's a piece of shit."

"Good thing you got out of there when you did. I don't think that's a good firm to work for."

I agreed, but apparently Bryan and I were in the minority, because the other law students had all flocked around the lawyers the second the presentation had finished. Foster had a large group around him--mostly women of course--and the attorneys from Cooper & Cooper had a captive audience hanging on their every word.

This evening had been a complete waste of time, and to cap it all off, Foster now knew I had lied about going on a date tonight.

Shit.

"Bryan?"

"Yeah?"

"Let's get out of here. I assume you don't want to network with any of these people?"

If we left together now, it might look like we were heading out for the evening on a date. Not a particularly romantic one, given that it had started with a networking event in law school, but a date nonetheless.

"Well actually, I wouldn't mind meeting Foster."

"I'll introduce you some other time. Come on, let's--"

"Hello April," Zach said, appearing out of nowhere in front of me. "I hope you were paying attention to what I said up there. You might actually learn something about being a lawyer."

"I don't intend to learn anything from you," I snapped back. "Now, if you'll excuse me, my date and I are just leaving."

Bryan frowned when he realized he was my date, but he was quick enough on the uptake to go along with it.

"How does Foster feel about that?" Zach asked. "Or have you moved on from him? It's so difficult to keep up with your men. One minute you're all over me, and the next you're ditching me for some thug in a suit."

"I was never 'all over you,' Zach. I never showed the slightest bit of interest. I respected you as a professional and that was it."

"Shame you're never going to become an attorney," Zach remarked. "All that hard work for nothing."

"I'm sure I'll be just fine. Come on, Bryan. Let's leave."

"You're screwed, April," Zach shouted loudly after us.

A few nearby students turned to look in our direction. I could have just carried on walking, but I didn't want him to keep shouting out comments about me as I left. Zach always had to get the last word in, but not this time.

"What are you babbling about?" I asked. "Just because I can't work at Cooper & Cooper, doesn't mean I'm never going to be a lawyer. I already have a new job at Arrington & Hedges."

"Yes, I know, and you've been working closely with Foster Arrington."

"So what?"

"You've fucked up, April. You've fucked up big time. I'm going to enjoy taking you down."

"Stop being so fucking cryptic and--"

"Is everything okay here?" Foster asked, appearing by my side just as he had done that night nine months ago.

"Everything's fine," I insisted. "We're just leaving."

"I was just telling your girlfriend that her career is never going to get off the ground," Zach said smugly. "She's fucked."

Given what happened the last time Zach had met Foster, he had a surprising amount of confidence, almost as if he had been drinking. He was certainly talking louder than I would have liked and now at least a third of the room was looking in our direction, having noticed that two of the lawyers were glaring at each other.

"I suggest you leave," Foster said quietly, but firmly, to Zach. "No one wants you here anyway."

"I'm not going anywhere," Zach replied.

"Do you remember what happened last time you didn't leave April alone? I'm happy to provide a reminder."

"You wouldn't dare," Zach yelled.

With every second that went passed, more and more people turned to look at us. These were my colleagues. The people I had to spend another year of law school with. I didn't want to spend the third year of law school as the girl two lawyers had a fight over at a public event.

Foster took a step forward towards Zach, narrowing the distance between them to just a foot.

"Please," I said, as I tried pointlessly to pull Foster back by the arm. I might as well have tried to pull down a brick wall.

"Go home, little man," Foster snarled.

At least he was keeping his voice down, but it didn't do a lot of good when everyone was crowding around us. Most people weren't even being subtle about it now. They were flat-out staring at us. At me.

"Tell your gorilla to step down, April," Zach said confidently, although I noticed that he took a step back to increase the distance between them.

Foster didn't move. He just stood there staring at Zach. I knew how powerful Foster's stare could be. Looking into those eyes had practically hypnotized me. If Foster could use those eyes to illicit fear as much as he could illicit desire, then Zach would be terrified right now.

Zach didn't seem perturbed by the audience. In fact, he was thriving off it, even though one of the partners from his law firm was in the same room. Clearly Zach felt he was invincible because of his father. He was probably right.

Zach looked around at the bemused law students surrounding him, and found a burst of confidence. Or stupidity. He lunged forward and thrust his hands into Foster's chest.

Foster barely flinched, but Zach stumbled back a few steps. Foster smiled and slowly walked right up to Zach and returned the favor. He planted his hands on Zach's chest and gave what looked like a completely effortless shove.

Zach went flying back. He managed to stay on his feet initially, but he couldn't regain his balance and ended up tumbling back into one of the tables containing what was left of the cheap buffet food. The table went crashing to the floor, and so did Zach, taking all the food with him.

There was no glass to break, but all the metal plates crashed to the floor, making a deafening noise in the process. A hundred people were now looking at me, whispering to each other and laughing.

The career counselor came over and tried to calm everyone down, but that just made the scene even more dramatic.

Foster tried to grab my arm, but I shook him off and fled the room. It was too late. Enough people had seen me at the center of the fight. By the time I started my third year of law school in August, everyone would know what had happened here tonight. I'd be a laughing stock.

"April, wait," Foster's yell followed me out of the room, echoing off the walls as I ran down the stairs and out into the yard at the front of the school.

As usual, there was nothing fresh about the air in D.C., even at night, but at least no one out here was laughing at me.

Maybe Zach was right. My law career would be over before I even knew it. I'd failed. All I'd wanted to do was follow in Mom's footsteps, so that she would be proud of me.

If she could see me now, she'd be embarrassed. Ashamed of what I'd become and how I'd made a mess of every opportunity that had come my way.

Sorry Mom. I tried, I really did.
Tried and failed.

Chapter Nineteen

FOSTER

I couldn't win. Even when I behaved myself I managed to mess everything up.

It had taken every ounce of willpower in me to not punch that guy. When he'd been talking during the panel, I'd wanted to strangle him just so that I wouldn't have to hear him speak.

I'd kept an eye on him after the panel, and sure enough he went over and spoke to April. She clearly didn't want to speak to him, but I let her deal with it. I was there to keep an eye on her, not fight all her battles for her.

But then something changed. I couldn't hear what they were saying, but he clearly threatened her and she looked distressed. The guy she was with didn't look too pleased with what he'd heard either.

My instincts had taken over at that point, but all I'd done was joined in the conversation and asked if everything was okay. If Zach had half a brain in his head he would have walked away and that would have been that.

The public often had a misconception that lawyers were intelligent, in addition to being money-sucking bastards. The truth was that lawyers came in all shapes and sizes. Graduating law school wasn't a challenge in itself, and some states' bar exams were laughably easy.

The hard bit was getting a job, and that process usually weeded out the morons. Unless daddy owned a law firm, of course. I still didn't count myself in that category, despite working for Mom's firm. I got head-hunted on a weekly basis. I was still at Arrington & Hedges in spite of Mom, not because of her.

April had run off after Zach had gone tumbling over the table and made a complete fool of himself. I'd hardly touched him. The push was supposed to be ironic. I'd only wanted to push him as pathetically as he'd pushed me, which I'd barely felt. I didn't know my own strength sometimes.

April probably wasn't mad at seeing Zach go flying. She just didn't like making a scene. April liked to blend into the background; she had no idea that was impossible for someone with her beauty.

It spoke to her modesty that she genuinely thought she was unremarkable. In reality, people stared at her whenever she entered a room, and in my case I couldn't take my eyes off her.

Now I had to make it up to her. Just when things between us had been heating up, I'd gone and put us back to square one.

April's friend had tried to run after her, but I'd stopped him and told him I would find her. He seemed like a nice guy, and just didn't like the idea of her walking around on her own late at night. That made two of us.

Her apartment was at least a fifteen minute walk away, but I knew D.C. better than most, and there were plenty of shortcuts back to her place for people who were prepared to walk through the less desirable parts of town.

Right now I'd walk over broken glass, so a few drug dealers hanging out on the corner, didn't pose a huge threat.

I made it to her apartment in just over ten minutes, although I was out of breath, and dripping in sweat. *Fuck this humidity.*

I waited outside her apartment and sure enough, five minutes later she walked up the street towards me. She kept touching her hand to her face, which I initially thought was her tucking her hair behind her ears, but as she got closer I noticed she was just trying to wipe away tears before entering the apartment building.

April didn't notice me until she almost walked into me while digging her keys out of her purse.

"What are you doing here?" she snarled.

Safe to say I wasn't in her good books right now, then.

"I wanted to make sure you made it home okay," I replied.

"Yeah, you're my knight in shining armor. I'm home now. Mission accomplished."

"Do I sense some animosity towards me?" I asked.

April opened the front door, but only made a half-hearted attempt to close the door in my face. I took that as an invitation to follow her inside.

"I guess there are some brain cells under all that muscle and testosterone," she replied as she called for the elevator.

"No one's ever accused me of being stupid."

April wouldn't look in my direction, but I could still tell she had been crying from the redness around her eyes, and the way she kept dabbing her face.

I'd never seen her like this. She'd been pretty cut up after the thing with Zach nine months ago, but she hadn't cried, and even though I'd made her mad a few times, she'd always kept her emotions in check.

Tonight I'd fucked up. Big time.

"Zach had it coming," I insisted.

The elevator arrived and we both stepped in.

"That's not the point. You humiliated me in front of my friends and colleagues. All because you could resist the urge to hit someone."

"I didn't hit him; I pushed him. He just happened to go down like a sack of shit."

"You still made a scene. As usual, you made tonight all about you. Why were you even there?"

"Your school invited me."

"So? You must get invited to loads of those events. I'm guessing you usually turn them down because you're too busy earning money."

"I saw Zach was on the list of speakers. I figured it would be a good idea to go in case--"

"In case what? I needed protecting? Get over yourself Foster. I don't need you to look after me."

We stepped off the elevator and I followed April to her room. She didn't want a scene, but if she thought I was just going to let her go without a fight then she had another thing coming.

"You looked like you were in trouble," I said, lowering my voice so that it didn't echo down the hall.

"I was handling it."

April turned, putting her back to the door, and finally facing me head on. She'd stopped crying now, but her eyes were still pools of sadness.

"Can I come in?" I asked. The words sounded foreign on my tongue. I didn't usually have to ask. Women would typically open the door and drag me through it.

"You need to leave," she said quietly.

"I don't want to leave you like this."

"You don't have a choice in the matter. There's nothing you can say or do--"

I grabbed the back of her head and pulled her towards me. Our lips clashed together awkwardly, but we quickly fell into the rhythm we'd found nine months ago.

My tongue parted her lips and found its way inside her mouth, where it met with the soft embrace of her own.

She was clearly still mad with me, even though she didn't resist the kiss. Her tongue pushed against mine as if she were trying to get it out of her mouth, however her arms remained down by her side, neither embracing me nor pushing me away, as I kept kissing her with all the pent-up frustration of the last few weeks finally coming to the surface.

Our lips eventually broke apart for air, but I didn't let go of her head, keeping her mouth less than an inch from mine. We both gasped and panted for air, as I pressed my body against hers, letting her feel my eagerness bursting through my pants.

My hand stroked the back of her thigh, until I reached the hemline of her skirt. I pulled it up and took a firm hold of her ass, pushing myself against her in the process.

"I want you, April," I groaned, as my fingertips moved down her ass crack towards her sweet folds. She gasped as my fingers lightly pressed against her asshole, and then moved on to her pussy, where I teased open the lips and found the entrance to paradise. "I want another night with you. How many times do I have to tell you?"

She kept her back to the door, but her hand fumbled with the key in the lock until she finally got it open.

The door opened.

This was it. After nine slow months without her, I would now go back to the sweet ecstasy that lie between her legs.

"No," she mumbled quietly. "I'm sorry. This can't happen."

She backed away from me, my fingers torn from her soft skin, as she walked into her apartment and closed the door behind her, taking my hopes of a beautiful night with her.

I rested my head against her door trying to think of anything that would direct blood away from my penis.

Zach. That did the trick nicely.

I left and headed home. I'd fucked it up. April wanted me--or at least, she wanted my body--but that wasn't enough for someone like her. All women wanted me to fuck them, and usually that was it. But not April. She needed more than that in a man.

She needed something I couldn't give her. I just wished I knew what it was.

Chapter Twenty

APRIL

Working at Foster's law firm did have some advantages. Summer associates were paid the same amount as first-year associates which meant I had gone from being a student having to live off loans to cover my living expenses, to suddenly earning $3,000 a week.

Even after tax, I earned more in a week than I ever had in a month before now. I'd always been embarrassed by my bank account, and I still was, but for a very different reason.

The amount of money Arrington & Hedges paid me was absurd, but it's not like I was going to give it back. Besides, it meant I could fly home to New York without having to worry about paying for the ticket or asking Dad for money, and right now what I really needed more than anything else in the world was to spend the weekend with Dad.

I texted him to let him know I was heading home and he replied telling me to go straight to Kathleen's New York place. I guess that meant he was living there full-time now. I couldn't really blame him. Given a choice between living in a mansion, or a small three-bedroom house that was falling apart, I would take the mansion as well.

Dad suspected something was wrong the second I'd told him about my visit. He usually had to beg me to come home, and I wasn't one for surprise visits. I put a brave face on--easy enough to do via text message--and told him I just wanted to get away from the stress of work for the weekend.

There was some truth to that. I wanted to get away from the office, because the office reminded me of Foster. So did my apartment. I couldn't spend any time in my bedroom without having flashbacks to that night nine months ago, and even the hallway now reminded me of a kiss I would rather forget.

Foster's touch made me weak at the knees. It didn't matter where on my body he touched me. This time he'd gone to my thigh and ass, but he could just as easily have held my hand or touched my back, he would have gotten the same reaction from me; a racing heart and a dripping wet sex.

The second I saw Dad, I couldn't keep up the pretense any longer. I looked up at him as he opened the door, smiled, and then burst into tears.

Dad laughed and brought me in for a hug.

"What's so funny?" I sobbed.

"You used to do that when you were a kid and you'd done something naughty," Dad replied. "You'd look up at me just as I was about to tell you off, and then you'd burst into tears."

"I remember."

"I'm sure you did it just so that I wouldn't punish you."

"It usually worked," I said, smiling. Dad and I went into the living room, and sat down on one of the soft leather sofa. "Is Kathleen around?"

"No, she's gone out to run some errands. We have time to talk. Are you going to tell me what's wrong?"

"I'm not sure I can talk to you about it."

"Boy trouble?"

I shook my head. I didn't want to talk about Foster right now, and I didn't think that was what had me so upset anyway. I wanted Foster and he wanted me. I'd felt that much digging into my stomach when we kissed. Why couldn't I let him in?

"Girl problems?" Dad guessed.

"You really want to talk about girl problems?" I joked.

"Well, it depends what they are. I have a small selection of speeches I can offer you based on what I've read in women's magazines. Let's see, are you having your first period?"

I laughed. "No, Dad, we're a little way past that one."

"Ah, okay. Is your period late?"

"Nope."

"Thank God for that. I think that's all I have memorized. Tell you what, why don't you describe the problem and I'll try to improvise?"

Where did I start? I wasn't happy at work. I was earning a small fortune. Dad would be giddy if he ever earned half of what they were paying me right now. But the work felt shallow and dry.

The only piece of work that seemed vaguely interesting and might have helped people was fighting the PorTupe fraud, but Foster had stopped me going anywhere near that. All because we had to keep the client happy, even when the client was a company run by awful people.

"Did Mom enjoy her job?" I asked.

Dad hesitated before answering, which I hadn't been expecting. "I'm not sure she enjoyed the work so much as she thrived off the pressure. She wouldn't have given it up for the world, but saying she enjoyed it is probably going a bit too far. We didn't talk about work much to be honest."

"Why not?"

"I didn't understand what she did, and she would often get stressed out just talking about it."

"She always seemed so happy when she spoke to me. Mom made it sound like the best job in the world, but now that I'm doing it I'm not so sure."

Dad smiled and wrapped his arm around my shoulders. "Have you ever asked a kid what they want to be when they grow up?"

"Yes, I guess so. Why?"

"They always give crazy answers, don't they? Like astronaut, or fireman, or actor. Do you know what you used to say when you were a kid?" I shook my head. "You said you wanted to be a lawyer like Mommy."

I smiled. I couldn't remember having said that, but it sounded like the kind of thing I would say. "Maybe the dream is better than the reality. I don't want to just be a lawyer. I want to be a great lawyer, like Mom."

"I know. And your mother always wanted to support you in that dream. But if you remember, she also always told you to find your own path. She told you to consider other areas of law. You don't have to do corporate law to make your mom proud, April. Hell, you don't have to do law at all if you don't want to."

"Mom made it look so easy."

"Yeah, she did didn't she. Your mother was quite the actress at times. She certainly had me fooled."

"What do you mean?"

I looked up into Dad's eyes and could see he was struggling to hold back tears as well. He always got emotional whenever we talked about Mom, but I'd never seen him cry before. He'd always been strong in front of me.

"April," Dad said softly, as he removed his arm from my shoulders, and turned around to look at me. "I need to tell you the truth about the accident that killed your mom."

Chapter Twenty-One

APRIL

The truth?

"I already know what happened, Dad. Mom died in a car crash."

"Yes, she did. But I kept some of the facts from you."

"Why?" What other facts could be important? My mom had been killed. Surely everything else paled into insignificance in comparison to that?

"Do you remember what life was like in the months before your mother died?"

I'd been sixteen when Mom died. Old enough to have reached the terrible teens with full force and effect. I'd spent more time arguing with my parents than talking to them, but all kids did that.

Dad had long ago convinced me that I didn't need to feel guilty for the way I'd acted towards Mom in the months before her death. From my point of view, I'd been a completely ungrateful bitch, but to Mom and Dad I'd just been a sulky teenager. Apparently they even used to laugh about it, because I was living up to such a cliché stereotype.

"I'd been a bit moody," I replied. "I don't remember why."

"A *bit* moody?" Dad said with a laugh. "That's the understatement of the century. Yes, you were a bit difficult to live with, however you weren't the only one with issues."

"You and Mom fought a few times," I said, as I remembered hearing them argue through the thin walls.

I usually had headphones on in my room because Dad got annoyed at the loud music, but sometimes I just lay on the bed and thought about boys from school. That's when I'd hear the arguments. I couldn't tell what they were arguing about, but it was impossible to ignore the angry, raised voices.

"Yes," Dad admitted. "There were arguments."

"Were you going to break up?"

"God no, nothing like that. We both loved each other very much. The rows were just because of the stress your mother was under. She started working later and later, often not coming home until midnight or the early hours of the morning."

"That's the job," I said. "I've experienced that already. When there's a big deal going down in the office, people start working all the hours available to get it finished."

"I know. I'm not completely insensitive to what she had to go through at work. However, when one big deal finished, another would start, and before you knew it she was working like that non-stop."

"I didn't realize," I said softly. Of course I didn't; I was too consumed with myself to pay attention to what my mother was going through. No doubt I'd been obsessed with some boy whose name I couldn't even remember anymore.

"Good," Dad said. "We didn't want you to worry about it. I tried to convince your mother to take a step back, and maybe even move jobs if necessary. We didn't need all that money, but your mom was an incredibly ambitious woman."

"I remember. She wanted to become managing partner one day."

"And she would have as well, of that I have no doubt. When your mother wanted something she got it."

"Like you?" I joked.

"Yes, like me," Dad said. "I was quite the catch back in the day. Your mother wasn't the only lady lining up for a bit of--"

"Okay Dad, I believe you. But what does all this have to do with Mom's death?"

The smile quickly disappeared from Dad's face. He'd let himself get sidetracked to delay having to break the news as long as possible.

"In the week leading up to the crash, things at work were absolutely crazy. I always liked to wait up for her, but she was getting in at one or two in the morning every day, including weekends. She often came home looking like a zombie."

"I can't imagine Mom looking haggard," I said. "She always looked radiant to me. Perhaps that's just the way I like to remember her."

"I think it just goes to show the wonders of modern makeup."

"If she was still alive, she'd kill you for that comment."

Dad smiled. "Yeah, she would, at that. I told her to work from home, but it wasn't so easy to do it in those days."

"Even now you have to show your face in the office all the time or people don't believe you're working."

"I can believe that. Law firms are so slow to evolve. Anyway, on the day of the accident, your mom left for work looking more exhausted than I'd ever seen her. She looked dead on her feet. I actually cried that

149

morning. It was like she was dying slowly in front of my eyes."

"I never even noticed," I whispered guiltily. "I had slept in that day. You had to wake me up to tell me what had happened."

Dad shook his head. "The accident didn't happen on her way to work. I know I told you it did, but that's not what happened."

"It's not?"

"No. At just gone four o'clock in the morning, your mom drove onto the wrong side of the road and slammed straight into an oncoming car. Fortunately the other driver survived, but your mom was killed instantly."

"It was her fault, wasn't it?" I asked. Dad nodded. "You told me she'd been hit by a kid driving too fast."

"I lied. She fell asleep at the wheel. At least, that's what we think happened. There were no drink or drugs in her system, and she hadn't been using her phone. She was exhausted. The job had driven her to the edge, and she'd toppled over."

"Why didn't you tell me?"

"You worshiped your mom," Dad said. "After the accident, you suddenly became studious and worked hard because you 'wanted to make Mom proud.' By the time I realized that meant you would become a lawyer as well, it was too late for me to say anything."

A year ago, Dad's revelation would have come as a huge shock, but now, after seeing what life was like at large law firms, I completely believed it. Mom had been made partner in record time, and you didn't achieve that by working nine to five, Monday to Friday.

"I don't know what to say," I muttered.

"Do you hate me for keeping this from you?"

"No, of course not." I gave my Dad a hug, which he looked like he desperately needed right now.

"I don't want you to think any less of your mom. She was still a remarkable woman."

"I know. And I don't. She didn't do it on purpose. It's almost a relief to know she wasn't superhuman."

"She can still be your hero, sweetie."

"She is. And so are you."

Dad wrapped his arm around me again and for a few minutes I just rested my head on his shoulder and closed my eyes.

Over the last ten years, I'd been so obsessed with making Mom proud of me that I'd never given a second thought to what would make Dad proud. He was the one who'd raised me by himself for the last of those teenage years, and supported me through college and now law school.

"Maybe I should give some more thought to my choice of career," I said, still laying on Dad's shoulder.

"You don't want to be a lawyer any more?"

"I'm not sure. I do enjoy legal writing, I just don't like the work I'm doing at the moment."

"Well don't rush into anything. You've spent a long time following this dream; don't ditch it on the spur of the moment."

"I won't."

I heard someone coming down the stairs and looked up expecting to see Kathleen. It wasn't her.

"Foster?"

"Hi." He stood in the doorway, as if unsure about coming into his own living room.

"What are you doing here?"

"I'm hanging out with some old friends this weekend and didn't fancy staying in a hotel."

Dad removed his arm from my shoulder, and stood up, yawning and stretching himself out as he did so. Dad always did that when he'd been sitting for a while. He'd never have been suited to an office job where you spent most of your time with your ass in a chair.

"I'll leave you kids to it," Dad said as he stretched his neck from side-to-side.

What did he mean by that? Leave us to it? Surely he couldn't know about what had happened between us? I hadn't even mentioned Foster yet.

"Actually, Mr. Rhodes," Foster said politely, "I'd like to speak to you for a moment if I may."

"Uh, okay, sure. But call me Pierce."

"Pierce," Foster said reluctantly, as if trying out a foreign word on his tongue. "I need to apologize. For my behavior last time I was here."

Dad looked down at me with a bemused expression on his face. I shrugged in response. I was as surprised as he was.

"Are you feeling okay, Foster?" I asked. "You're in danger of sounding like a reasonable person."

"April," Dad scolded. "Don't be rude. It's not easy for Foster to apologize."

"I am sorry," Foster said sincerely. "I shouldn't have said those things about you just being with Mom for her money."

"So you don't think that anymore?" Dad asked.

"Oh yes, I still think you're just marrying her for the money. But I shouldn't have said that."

"That's a shitty apology," I snapped. "Why even bother?"

Dad just laughed. I loved how easy going he was, but I wished he would get mad sometimes as well.

"Calm down, April," Dad said. "Foster can't help what he thinks. The important thing is that he's polite." Dad turned his attention back to Foster. "I don't care if you don't like me, I just want you to act like you do in front of your mother because it means a lot to her that we get on."

"That sounds fair," Foster said.

"No it doesn't," I yelled. "Dad's not like that. I don't know why you think so badly of him."

"It's human nature, April," Dad said soothingly. "My in-laws hated me for years before I finally won them round."

"They did?"

"God yes. When your mother brought me back to meet them, they thought she was just going through a phase. I was her 'bit of rough.'"

I cringed, and did my best not to think of my dad as anyone's 'bit of rough.' That was especially difficult bearing in mind that my own bit of rough was standing just ten feet away.

"If it makes you feel any better," Dad continued, "we have both signed a pre-nup."

"You have?" Foster asked, looking surprised.

"Yep. So you don't need to worry about me stealing all your mom's money."

"Thanks," Foster said, nodding his head in what I took as a sign of respect towards Dad. There was some hope for that relationship yet. "Okay, I'm going to go hang out in my room."

Foster looked at me and winked. I glared at him, but Dad had been too busy turning on the television to notice. Same old Foster. We had barely spoken since he'd tried to kiss me in the hallway, but clearly he wasn't going to let me forget.

"Will you both be in for dinner?" Dad asked. Foster and I both nodded. "Good. We should have a big meal together tonight. Kathleen and I have an announcement to make."

"Great," Foster replied dryly. "I'm looking forward to it already."

Foster headed up to his room, but I didn't follow him. I didn't trust myself to be alone with him in his bedroom. Not after what happened the other night.

I wanted to believe Foster had changed, but he'd shown no remorse for embarrassing me that evening.

Apologizing to Dad had been a nice thing to do though, even if it wasn't exactly the most groveling apology ever.

At least Dad was happy. That was a start. He hadn't looked this happy since Mom died. I curled up on the sofa and rested my feet on Dad's lap. He'd put some crappy car show on the television, but I didn't care. Right now, I just wanted to hang out with my dad.

Chapter Twenty-Two

FOSTER

That had been painful.

I tried to think of another time in my life where I had apologized to someone, but nothing came to mind. I wasn't really the apologizing type. I'd never had a girlfriend to grovel to. If a woman demanded I apologize for something I'd done then she was quickly shown the door. I didn't need that shit in my life.

So why had I apologized to Pierce? Certainly not because I cared about him. And, if I'm honest, I hadn't done it to please my mother either. I'd done it to impress the one girl I felt the need to make amends with.

I strolled up the stairs towards my room. April might come up and join me, but I didn't like my chances. Being nice to her dad was just the first step of what would probably be an entire staircase's worth of them.

I nearly walked into Mom standing at the top of the stairs. She looked pleased with herself.

"I heard what you said in there," she said, grinning at me. "That was a very nice thing to do."

I tried to shrug casually, but that wasn't an easy thing to pull off for a guy of my size. "I just don't want there to be any awkwardness between us. If we have to spend time together we need to at least be civil."

"That's surprisingly mature of you."

"Yeah, who'd have thought it."

"I meant what I said about Pierce. He's a good man, and I can assure you he's not in this relationship for my money."

"I know. He told me about the pre-nup."

Mom looked downstairs to check the coast was clear and then motioned for me to follow her into my room.

"The pre-nup is for Pierce's benefit not mine," Mom said quietly.

"Oh for God's sake. Please don't tell me you've signed away all your money to him? You know, pre-nups are supposed to *preserve* the wealth of the rich spouse, not piss it all away."

"And that's exactly what this pre-nup is doing," Mom replied. "I have more than enough money to look after myself, and you, if you need it, well into retirement. And so does Pierce."

I raised my eyebrows, and gave Mom a dismissive look. "No offense, but I can't imagine a security guard really earns a fraction of the amount you do."

"No he doesn't, but he still has a small fortune tucked away."

"Did he win the lottery or something?"

I knew April had gone to the school that had given her the best scholarship offer, so if Pierce had come into money then it had either been a very recent thing, or April just didn't know about it.

"Not exactly. He came into money, but paid a heavy price for it."

"Spit it out, Mom. I have to be back at work in two days."

"You have to promise not to tell April."

"Fine," I replied. "It's not like we're close anyway."

"I'm not so sure about that." I opened my mouth to refute her insinuation, but she carried on talking. "When Pierce's wife died, she was a partner at a large law firm. Unlike your father, she also had generous life insurance. She was insured up to her eyeballs. Pierce received the full payout and tucked it away in a savings account. He's sensible like that."

Life insurance. How could I have missed that. Even as just an associate, I had life insurance that would pay out a large multiple of my salary on my death. For someone like April's mom, that would have been many millions.

Unfortunately, Dad's life wouldn't have been worth insuring. He'd rarely worked, and when he did it tended to be cash in hand. As much as I missed my father's presence and emotional support, the loss of his financial contribution hadn't had much effect.

"Why doesn't April know?" I asked. "I'm surprised Pierce didn't pay for college and law school for her."

"He'll pay off that debt when the time comes. Pierce just wanted her to make her own decisions like a normal kid. Pierce grew up in a poor family that could barely put food on the table. He doesn't even know what to do with that amount of money. I'm sure he'll tell her when he thinks the time is right."

"That means she doesn't have to become a corporate lawyer," I said. "She can do whatever she wants."

"And she wants to be a corporate lawyer," Mom replied. "Let her make her own way."

"I'm not so sure."

April had proven herself to be an excellent attorney already and she hadn't even graduated law school yet, but I didn't think she enjoyed the work. That might not be a huge problem for one summer, but if she was going to do this the rest of her life she needed to get more out of it.

"You can't tell her, Foster. It's none of our business. I only told you so that you'll stop giving Pierce a hard time."

"Fine. The secret is safe with me."

"Good. Now, talking about secrets, I'm hearing a lot of talk about you and April spending time together late at the office and--"

"Kathleen?" Pierce yelled out from the bottom of the stairs with perfect timing. "We should hit the shops and get food for tonight."

"We'll talk about this later," Mom said, as she disappeared down the stairs.

Not if I can help it.

Mom and Pierce left to go shopping, and shortly after I heard April come up the stairs. Her footsteps approached my room, but she kept on walking and entered the spare room next door that Mom had reserved for her.

I wasn't going to win her over by sitting in my room alone. I got up and walked to the room next door. The room that had previously been a spare room that I hogged for playing video games as a kid. Now it had my workout bench and a scattering of weights.

"Come in," April said softly after I knocked on the door.

"How's your new room?" I asked, walking in and looking around at the familiar, yet strange, room.

The weights had all been shoved under the bed, and the workout bench was pushed up against a wall in the corner. The old desk was still there, except instead of being used for a television and video game console, it now just had a computer.

April stood with her back to me examining some makeup that had been left on the chest of drawers. Mom, or maybe Pierce, had tried to make the place feel like a home away from home, but April looked a little overwhelmed by it all.

"Your mom's really nice," April said. "She's spent a fortune on all this stuff."

"She just doesn't want to see you without makeup on. It's not a pretty sight."

Smooth, Foster, real smooth.

April turned around, but instead of giving me a death stare, she broke into a smile. "How would you know what I look like without makeup on? You left before I woke up, remember?"

I knew exactly what she looked like without makeup. I'd woken up about six in the morning that day, and had quickly gotten dressed and stolen her panties as I always did after a one-night stand.

The blinds in her apartment were cheap and didn't keep out much of the light. The early morning sun had shone on the bed, illuminating April's face in a soft orange glow.

She'd been captivating even without the makeup, which she must have removed while I'd been recovering from one of our many sessions that night. I'd almost undressed and crawled back into bed. As it was, I stared at her for at least ten minutes, before finally tearing myself away.

"Maybe next time I'll stick around until the morning," I replied.

She smiled again, but didn't respond. Was that a good thing or a bad thing?

"Thank you for what you said to my dad," April said, as she sat down on the new double bed that was also a new addition to the room. "That meant a lot to both of us."

"I think I need to apologize for the bad apology," I joked. "I didn't exactly knock that one out of the park."

"It just takes practice. I'm sure you'll get plenty of that."

"Yeah, I think you might be right."

"You can sit down," she said, patting the bed next to her. "Judging by the wallpaper and the weights under the bed, I'm guessing you used to spend a lot of time in this room."

"I've had some fun times in here."

"I probably don't want to know."

I grinned. "Nothing sordid, thank you very much. I saved that for the bedroom."

April opened her mouth to speak, changed her mind, opened it again, and finally closed it.

"What is it?" I asked. "You obviously want to say something."

"It's a little personal."

"I've seen you naked. I've felt you orgasm on my cock. I think we're beyond personal."

"Good point. Your Dad. What happened to him?"

"Cancer," I replied. "Lung cancer. He was relatively young, but he'd smoked since he was a teenager. Can't say he didn't bring it upon himself, but that doesn't make it any easier to bear."

April laughed gently. "Tell me about it."

"Now I get to ask you a question."

"I'm not going to like this am I?"

"Probably not," I admitted. "But I'm going to ask it anyway. Why did you bail on me the other night outside your apartment? I know you wanted me. You were dying for it as much as I was."

April looked down at her lap and took a few moments to compose herself before answering. Either that, or she was thinking up a lie. I didn't know which.

"I'm sure we would have had a good night," April said. "But there's no way this can end well. It's bad enough that you're my boss--"

"I won't be for much longer."

"No, but after the summer you will be my stepbrother. This won't have a happy ending."

"I'm fairly sure there was a happy ending the last time we spent the night together. More than one actually."

"I guess I can't deny that."

"Nope. Look, I know the sensible version of you thinks this is an awful idea, but there's another part of you that is desperate to go through with this. Where's the April that brought a stranger back to her apartment that night?"

"Well, you're not a stranger anymore, so it's no fun."

April smiled, but it disappeared quickly when I looked into her eyes. She held my gaze, even as I lifted my hand to her cheek and lightly brushed her soft skin.

Then I kissed her.

Chapter Twenty-Three

FOSTER

Her hands went straight to my chest, but instead of pushing me away, her fingers dug into my muscles through the thin cotton t-shirt that was stretched over my pecs.

She'd been wanting to do that for a long time.

I quickly unbuttoned her blouse before she could have a change of heart. Her sexy light blue bra, covered in a lacy trim, pushed up her chest so that her two breasts looked like fresh fruit ripe to be squeezed. That's exactly what I did.

What had started as a soft kiss, had quickly turned aggressive, as our hands grabbed at each other's bodies to claim what we'd both been wanting all this time. My hand popped round to her back and gracefully opened the bra with one flick of my fingers, before I practically tore the blouse and bra from her body.

"What if our parents come home?" April asked. I could tell she was just going through the motions. She wouldn't have stopped right now even if they were in the next room.

"They won't be home for at least an hour."

My lips went down to her breasts where I sucked greedily at her nipples, and bit down gently with my teeth, claiming her breasts as my property. She whimpered slightly, but held my head to her chest.

This time it's happening.

She clawed at my t-shirt until I had to move my head from her chest for her to pull it off completely. April looked at my chest with a hungry look in her eyes, much like I had when I stared at her.

I thrust my hand between her legs, reaching up her skirt until I felt the soft cotton of her damp panties. I pressed my palm against her sex, covering every inch of her folds and applying gentle pressure to her clit.

April groaned and locked her mouth against mine for an aggressive embrace. Her fingers gripped my back as she squirmed under my touch. April might be shy at the office, but once I got her naked the animal inside always came out.

When my fingers weaved their way under her panties and into her wet pussy, April pulled away from my lips and fell back onto the bed. I looked down at her perfect breasts, each topped off with erect nipples like the cherry on a cake, as she wriggled around while I finger-fucked her tight sex.

I was about to pull her skirt off and go down between her legs when I felt the familiar convulsions of her muscles clamping around my fingers. She was about to come hard, and I wasn't about to interrupt her, even if it meant missing out on tasting that gorgeous pussy for the time being.

I shoved my two fingers deep insider her, curling them slightly to rub the sensitive spot on the top of her tunnel, before pulling them almost the entire way out and then thrusting them back inside.

"Come for me," I moaned.

My command was well received. Her fingers grabbed hold of the bed spread as her back arched into the air. Her muscles spasmed around my fingers as she came, leaving them covered in her essence.

I removed her skirt and peeled off her soaking wet panties so I could get a good look at her naked and glowing on the bed. This was almost better than the actual sex. Almost.

"I like it when you boss me around," April said as she lay on the bed gasping for breath. "Especially when you order me to come for you."

Music to my ears. "You want to give you some more orders?"

April leaned up onto her elbows and bit her lip in that sexy, innocent way she could somehow still pull off even when she was lying naked with her cum pooling between her thighs.

"Yes, please," she replied. "Tell me what to do."

I stood up and unbuckled my jeans, before letting them drop to the floor. I kicked them off and then did the same with my boxers. April stared directly at my cock as if she wasn't sure it was real. I'd seen that look before many times, but fortunately there was one sure way to prove to a woman just how real it was.

"Get on your knees," I ordered.

April barely hesitated. She grabbed a pillow from the bed and threw it in front of my before dropping down to her knees. The pillow was a nice touch--I had to respect a woman who knew how to avoid carpet burn.

"Now what?" she teased. "I'm not sure I know what to do here?"

I grabbed the back of her head, weaving my fingers into her luscious blonde hair, and used my other hand to angle my rock hard cock down towards her tender lips. The pre-cum glistened on the tip, waiting for her to lick it clean.

"Suck," I said firmly. "And don't be all ladylike about it either."

I hadn't expected her to take my command so seriously. She immediately opened her mouth and clamped her lips around my cock, going down as far as she could manage, before coming back up with a loud slurping noise.

The amount of suction she applied to my cock was fucking insane. Her hand grabbed the base of my shaft to stroke the part she couldn't reach with her mouth, while she kept sucking hard at the rest of it like it contained the secret to everlasting life.

I could come right now. I could easily explode into her mouth. I placed a second hand on the back of her head, and started pulling her down onto my cock.

She pressed her hands against my thighs for support but she didn't fight me. When I let go, she came up desperate for air, but then went straight back down onto my shaft, which was now covered in her saliva.

I didn't want to come yet, but I couldn't fight the desire to keep fucking her mouth. Every time I looked down and saw her cute little face doing a number on my cock, I thought I had died and gone to heaven.

Just seconds before I exploded, I pulled her head off my cock and held it a foot from me, fighting her desperate attempts to get her lips back around it.

Shit, if I'd known she was this hungry for cock, I might never have walked out on her nine months ago.

I left her on her knees as I ran back to my bedroom to grab a condom. I arrived back in her room fully sheathed and ready to pound that wet pussy like there was no tomorrow.

April had gone back to the bed and was now on all fours, her perfect little ass wiggling in my direction just waiting for me to come and claim her.

"My sex sense told me your next order would be for me to get on my hands and knees," April said, looking round at me with a cheeky grin.

I took a few deep breaths to calm myself down and walked slowly over to the bed. Her pussy lips were still wet with her essence, as I clambered onto the bed and positioned myself between her open legs.

While I was busy admiring the view, April's hand reached back and grabbed hold of my shaft, positioning the tip against her entrance.

"Someone's keen to make up for lost time," I teased.

"Don't make me beg again. Just fuck me."

"Yes, ma'am," I replied. I plunged my cock all the way inside her in one smooth motion. She was already dripping wet from her last orgasm, so I slipped in with ease and was rewarded with a deep groan of pleasure as April sunk her head forward onto the pillow.

I gripped her hips and fucked her hard. We both knew it couldn't last long, but it didn't need to, we were both so close to the edge.

April greeted each thrust with a different noise, letting out whatever came naturally in a way that could never be faked.

I tried slowing down at one point to draw out the experience, but April just rocked her ass back into me and ordered me to keep fucking her. I don't know when it changed from me giving the orders to her, but I couldn't exactly complain.

The moans turned to a whimper and then a whine, as her body stiffened, each muscle going hard, before she started shaking uncontrollably. I kept fucking her; clearly I was doing something right, so I wasn't about to stop.

She hadn't even finished coming when I grabbed hold of her hair, gave her one final thrust, and then emptied myself inside her. I left my cock inside her while she continued spasming from her orgasm, until we both collapsed down on the bed in a sweaty, satisfied pile.

We were both too exhausted to have the whole conversation about feelings, dating, and the future, and we had to get dressed in case our parents came home. We did discuss one important point though--we wouldn't wait nine months before doing that again.

-*-

Mom knew. I was sure of it. She'd nearly confronted me about it before Pierce's timely interruption, but if she'd been in any doubt then she would have picked up on it over dinner.

April and I tried to act completely normal, but the tension between us had clearly cooled. Mom picked up on it immediately. Pierce commented on how nice it was to see us getting along, which I took to mean he didn't have a clue. Mom sat there stoic and silent. Yeah, she knew.

It didn't help that April had that "I've just been fucked by a big cock and had multiple orgasms" look about her either. There wasn't much she could do to hide it. Her face glowed and everything made her laugh or smile. I probably always had that effect on women, but I wasn't usually around to see it.

"Dad said you had some big news to give us tonight?" April asked, as we neared the end of dinner. "Good news I hope?"

"Mom, if you're pregnant, I swear to God--"

"Oh don't be silly Foster. I'm not pregnant, although I certainly could be the amount Pierce and I have been--"

"Kathleen, don't wind them up," Pierce said, once again speaking up to save me from a pain worse than death.

"Well, I've had to listen to enough of his escapades over the years. This is my revenge."

168

April looked uncomfortable. She didn't like talking, or even thinking about, my past history with women. We'd broached the subject briefly in bed together, but she'd quickly changed the subject.

We'd have to have the conversation soon. Two things had become clear this afternoon. One, we were going to do that again. Two, I desperately needed to come inside her tight pussy. Condoms didn't usually bother me, and I enjoyed seeing my cum splattered all over a woman's chest and face, so it had never been an issue before. But with April, I just felt a desperate urge to fill her with my seed. That had to happen soon.

"Let's tell them now," Pierce said, putting down his knife and fork.

"You sure you don't want to pour some drinks first?" Mom asked.

"They'll be fine," Pierce insisted. "I think they might even be relieved."

"Okay," Mom said reluctantly. "As you know, Pierce and I spent some time away together recently. We went hiked a lot and generally had an awesome time."

"I noticed you hadn't been at the office much recently," I said. "You planning on early retirement."

"No, not exactly. Anyway, we went to a lodge by Lake Tahoe for a while to chill out and while we were there we decided to get married."

"You've already told us you're getting married," April said. "How is that news?"

"She means, we decided to get married right there and then," Pierce said. "So we did. We're already married."

The news was greeted with a stunned silence. Kathleen and Pierce both looked at each other and then at me and April waiting for a response.

"Does this mean we don't have to sit through a wedding?" I asked. "Or are you still going to have a ceremony?"

"Nope, no ceremony," Mom said. "That's it. All done."

"Oh. Well, in that case, that is good news. No offense, but I wasn't exactly looking forward to sitting through all that. This seems like a good way to get it all over with."

"We didn't really see it as something to 'get over with,' " Mom said. "But I'm glad you're okay with it."

"What about you, April?" Pierce asked his daughter.

April hadn't said a word, and when I looked at her, I could see why. She looked like she was about to throw up. Her skin had turned a deathly shade of white; quite the contrast from the previous pink blush she'd had on show since the moment we'd started kissing in her room.

"Excuse me," April said solemnly, standing up and leaving the table. "I'm done eating. Congratulations."

Pierce went to stand up, but I stopped him. "Let me go and talk to her. I'm in a similar position to her after all."

Just when I thought we'd finally got things figured out. Nothing was ever easy with women. Why had I let myself fall for April? That's what had happened, there was no doubt about it.

I'd fallen for her. Fallen for her hard.

Chapter Twenty-Four

APRIL

I flew back to D.C. on Sunday night, but Foster's flight wasn't until Monday morning. That was for the best; we needed the time apart.

The news of Dad's marriage had hit me hard. Dad thought it was just the shock at knowing he was now married again, but that had nothing to do with it. Okay, maybe it had a little bit to do with it, but not a lot.

The real problem was Foster, or more specifically, what I'd done with Foster just a few hours before we'd gotten the surprise news about our parents' marriage.

I'd had weeks to accept the fact that Foster was going to be my new stepbrother, but I'd been so busy thinking of him as my annoying boss, that the longer-term problem had taken a back seat.

I think a part of me always thought Dad and Kathleen would call off the wedding at some point. I didn't resent them getting married, but it had seemed like a whirlwind romance, and those often fell apart.

Kathleen had been talking about arranging a huge marriage which would take at least a year to prepare. A year was a long time for a relationship. Even if they hadn't broken up, it would at least have meant Foster and I had time to get ourselves sorted out.

Now we'd fucked. And we were fucked.

Maybe it had been worth it. The sex had certainly been mind-blowing. My memories of our night together nine months ago, had the fog around them that was typical of alcohol-fueled encounters.

This weekend I'd been one-hundred-percent sober, and I had the crystal-clear memories to go with it. I could remember every single second of that afternoon. He'd made me come within a few short minutes using just his fingers, and then I'd devoured him with my mouth. Foster had told me after the sex that he'd had no idea I could suck cock like that. That made two of us.

Foster had then taken me roughly from behind exactly as I'd wanted. He could read my mind; that was the only possible explanation for the way he could hit exactly the right spot every single time. I couldn't finish myself off half as quickly as he'd managed it. He knew my body better than I did.

The travel and general stress of the weekend had left me exhausted, and the coffee they served in the office was completely inadequate for what I needed right now. Bryan agreed to meet up for coffee--he rarely took much persuasion, especially on Monday mornings--so I snuck out of the office at eleven and bought some much needed caffeine.

"I mean this in the nicest possible way," Bryan said as we sat down in the uncomfortable metal chairs, "but you look like crap."

"Thanks. I had a long weekend." I tried to take a sip of the coffee even though I knew it was far too hot, and then placed it down on the uneven table.

"A long weekend, as in you spent the whole time having fun and partying? Or as in you had to work the entire time?"

"Neither. I went back to New York to hang out with Dad."

"Oh, well that sounds nice. How was it?"

"It was... eventful."

"Are you going to keep me guessing all day?" Bryan asked. "Because even us government workers have to show our face in the office occasionally."

"Sorry," I replied taking a deep breath. I tried to take a sip of my coffee again, but it was still too hot. I wished the stuff could just be pumped directly into my veins, so that I didn't have to wait for it to reach a drinkable temperature. "My dad got married this weekend. Actually, he got married about a week ago, but he sprung the news on me as a surprise."

"Holy shit," Bryan exclaimed. "Yeah, that counts as an eventful weekend. I didn't realize they were going to get married so quickly."

"That makes two of us."

"At least you won't struggle for a job after law school," Bryan pointed out. "Your stepmother is the managing partner of a large law firm. That's pretty cool. I can see why this is difficult for you though. What with the tension between you and Foster."

Bryan had been front and center when Foster did his thing and protected me from Zach. There didn't seem to be much point denying our relationship.

"It's not just tension between us anymore," I admitted guiltily. "We kind of went past that."

I told Bryan what happened nine months ago, and this past weekend. It was a huge relief to get it off my chest, although I felt sick to the stomach when I imagined having to give the same speech to my dad at some point.

"So what's the situation between you now?" Bryan asked. "Are you dating?"

"No. I don't think so. We kind of left things in a bad place. I took the news of the marriage badly. He

173

assured me that it didn't make a difference, but I insisted on spending some time alone."

"Probably for the best. I think he's right though. From the sounds of it, you and he... you know... 'dated' before you even knew that your dad and his mom were a thing. It's no one's fault. Just bad luck."

"That's what he said."

"I may not have his body, or looks, but at least we are alike in some ways."

"Thanks Bryan. You always say the right thing."

"Pleasure. Look, I'd probably better be getting back to the office. Are you going to be okay?"

I nodded. "Yes. I'll be fine. Honestly."

I grabbed my coffee, which was now finally cool enough to drink, and headed back to the office. Foster would be in around lunchtime and for once I couldn't wait to see him. We had to talk, but I felt confident we could work this out.

Just before I entered the office building, my phone rang with an incoming call. I answered it immediately assuming it was Foster, but the voice on the other end of the phone was not one I wanted to hear.

"Hello April," Zach said, in his cocky, snide tone of voice. "I think it's about time we talk."

Chapter Twenty-Five

FOSTER

Nothing worth having was ever easy.

I'd heard people say that many times before, but never thought it applied to me. Most things I wanted in life had come easily to me. If I wanted a woman, ninety-nine times out of a hundred I got them. I blamed the other time on her husband coming home early.

Even becoming a lawyer had been a walk in the park. My college GPA had been good enough to graduate *magna cum laude*, and I'd just shown up for the LSAT and aced it. Law school had provided little in the way of challenge. I went to most of the classes that started after twelve, did some of the readings, nailed the exams, and took my pick of job offers after law school.

Now I had a challenge, and she went by the name of April.

She'd not taken the news of our parents' marriage too well. It'd had been a weird day. We'd spent an hour in bed together having the best sex of our lives, and then had to sit at the table looking at the newlyweds.

I calmed her down after dinner, but then I gave her space to think things through. I didn't panic. It had taken us a long time to get back in bed together and it was going to take a lot more than our parents early marriage to knock us off track now.

By the time she left for her flight on Sunday afternoon, we'd already resumed flirting whenever we had a modicum of privacy. I just had to remain patient and not rush things.

My phone was already ringing when I strolled into my office just before lunch. The caller showed up as "Cooper & Cooper," a name I knew all too well. None of the cases on my plate involved working with or against Cooper & Cooper, so they had no real reason to be calling me.

Intrigue got the better of me and I answered the call on speaker. I recognized the voice immediately.

"Hello Foster," Zach said on the other end of the phone. He couldn't even say hello without sounding like the type of cocky bastard I wanted to punch. "How are things?"

"Fine until I heard your voice," I replied. "What the hell do you want?"

I'd only met Zach twice in person and on those occasions he'd ended up getting punched, falling down the stairs, and collapsing into a table covered in food. You'd think he would have taken the hint and stayed the hell away. Perhaps that's why this conversation was taking place over the phone.

"I'm just calling about our mutual friend," Zach said. "I'm concerned about April's future as an attorney."

"April is not your friend. I would say you're more her enemy, but I'm not sure she's even given you a second thought. You're nothing to her."

"I wouldn't be so sure about that. You should see the picture she just sent me. But never mind about that. Like I said, I'm worried about April."

Picture? What picture? I was determined not to rise to his bait. That's exactly what he wanted, and it's exactly what April wouldn't want.

"Go on then, give your little speech," I said, hitting some buttons on my keyboard to make it sound like I was doing something more important. "Hurry up about it though. I'm pretty busy."

"That's good to hear. Perhaps you would like to pass along one of your major clients to me. You know, to help reduce your workload."

"Why on Earth would I do that? My clients want to be served by a reputable and, dare I say it, fucking awesome attorney. That's what they have with me."

"You'd be doing it for April," Zach said.

"Explain." This little shit just loved hearing himself talk. I'd been on the other end of the phone with attorneys like him before. It helped pad out the bill, but it was boring as hell.

"That was a good little speech you gave the other day at the law school. I didn't realize you worked for Jacob Oscar's company?"

"What of it?"

"Did April help you with any of that work?" Zach asked.

I thought back to the panel discussion. I'd definitely mentioned working for Jacob's company and I'd made it clear that a female summer associate had done some phenomenal work. It had given the law students in the room a confidence boost to know they could jump straight in at the deep end to do great legal writing.

"April helped," I replied. There didn't seem much point in denying it, because April was the only summer associate at the firm.

"Thought so," Zach said, before going quiet.

The silence on the other end of the phone unnerved me somewhat. I'd told him what he wanted to hear, but I couldn't for the life of me figure out what was the big deal. It wasn't a secret that I worked for Jacob; our firm's name was all over the SEC filings his company had submitted over the last few years.

"Is that all you wanted?" I asked. "Like I said, I am rather busy. If you ever become a competent lawyer you might find out what that's like."

"She's fucked up," Zach said smugly. "April's fucked up big time and if you don't give me PorTupe I'm going to take you both down."

"Yeah, yeah," I said, trying to sound calm. I could smell bullshit a mile off, but this wasn't it. Zach at the very least thought he had something on April, and his confidence had me worried. "Is that all you wanted? I'm actually busy with work for PorTupe right now. Those hundreds of thousands of dollars in annual billings don't just appear out of nowhere."

"I suggest you start wrapping up that project," Zach said. "Maybe mention to the board that they may want to seek new counsel. Think up an excuse, or just outright lie."

"I'm not going to do that."

"Then April will never even be admitted to the bar. I'll be in touch."

I always took calls on speakerphone in case I needed to type or write while on the call, but now I had nothing to slam down in frustration. I picked up the phone and slammed it back down anyway, but it didn't feel nearly as satisfying.

April knocked on the door. I knew it was her because she always knocked four times in the same unique way. One knock, followed by two quick knocks, finished off by another knock. There wasn't much she could do that wasn't adorable.

"Everything okay?" she asked as she walked in. "I heard you slam the phone down."

"I had a call from Zach," I said. "He mentioned something about you sending him photos."

"He called you as well?"

"Yes. Now, what's this about these photos."

April laughed, but said something that didn't sound at all funny. "He demanded that I send him a picture of my breasts, so I sent him one."

"You did what? Why did you do that?"

What the hell had she been thinking? Did Zach really have something that big on her?

"Calm down. Look, here's the picture I sent him."

April handed me her phone and I stared at a picture of what was definitely not her breasts. "These are your knees."

"Yep. I'm glad *you* know the difference. Zach doesn't appear to. I take a strange satisfaction from knowing that he's probably knocking one out to a picture of my knees."

I forced a laugh, but I didn't take this matter as lightly as April clearly did. Zach was demanding one of my clients. Not just any old client; my biggest client by far. Some years we billed them a million dollars. They'd be hard to replace.

"Why is he trying to blackmail you?" I asked. "At the networking event he mentioned having dirt on you, but I don't understand what he means."

"That makes two of us," April replied. "I don't know and I don't care. He's just bluffing, but I figured I'd string him along for a bit."

"Okay, well let me know if he calls again."

He will. I know he will. Whatever he's playing at, he's not yet finished.

"Will do."

"Not that I'm complaining, but why are you in my office?" I asked. "And why are you fully dressed?"

"I'm fully dressed because your office is freezing as per usual. And I'm here for business, not pleasure."

"Ugh. Okay, what is it?"

"It's about PorTupe."

First Zach, and now April. What was the obsession everyone had with that client? Oh yeah, the massive amount of legal bills they paid every year.

"What about them?"

"I've been doing some research online, and it turns out that there are loads of stories of people being discriminated against by PorTupe. People have even lost their jobs because of race or gender."

"There are also stories online about UFOs, Bigfoot, and the Star Wars prequels actually being good movies. Don't believe everything you read."

"You're a Star Wars fan?"

"I like to think I can handle a lightsaber."

April smirked, pursing her lips together tightly, and I thought back to how she'd had them clamped around my cock a few days ago. How would I ever get any work done with her across the hall?

"These aren't just silly stories," April continued. "There's a pattern. People make claims, but then drop the suit. In some cases it sounds like there were threats made by the company against the former employees, but other cases just settled. The details are a little thin because there are non-disclosure agreements involved."

"And if this is true, those NDAs are being broken by talking about the cases online."

"*That's* what you think is important here?" April asked incredulously. "A broken NDA?"

"My point is that perhaps people who are breaking a legally binding confidentiality agreement shouldn't be considered all that trustworthy."

"Where there's smoke there's fire," April replied.

"No, where there's smoke there's smoke. Smoke is generated by many different chemical reactions, not just fire."

April groaned through gritted teeth. "You're impossible sometimes, you know that?"

"What do you want me to do, April? They're my client. I do the work they ask me to do. And you know what, if they ask me to defend them on a discrimination lawsuit then I'll do that as well."

"Don't expect me to help you," April replied. "I just can't do that kind of work."

"You'll do the work you're given."

April pouted and crossed her arms over her chest. I did my best to look mad and not aroused, but she made it fucking difficult sometimes. She could act like a petulant child, and I still couldn't be angry with her, not really.

"Speaking of work," I said. "Mom thinks it's a good idea for you to give a presentation to the firm. Most of your work has been for me, but I won't be making the decision about whether or not to offer you a job after the summer. You need to impress the partners."

"Fine, I can do that. As long as I don't have to give a speech arguing the merits of discriminating against people."

"I've picked out the topic for you. The Delaware Court of Chancery has handed down a big decision on poison pills used to prevent hostile takeovers. I want you to compare it to the current leading authority and talk about what might change with this new precedent. I've emailed you all the details."

"Thanks. Guess I better get going."

"Oh April," I called out just as she was about to open the door. She turned to glare at me and I blew her a kiss. When did I become a soppy romantic?

April stared at me for a few seconds, but finally smiled and blew me a kiss in return.

I did feel a little guilty about setting her up with this presentation, but I'd put the wheels in place when she'd dumped all that *pro bono* work on my plate.

April had a sense of humor, but she also embarrassed easily. This might get me in a lot of trouble.

Chapter Twenty-Six

APRIL

I'm going to kill him.

Preparing the presentation had been easy. Both the cases were written by a judge capable of writing in clear English, and even the 'old' case was only written ten years ago. There was no archaic language and no difficult concepts to grasp.

It also helped that I'd taken a Corporations class this year, so the law on poison pills was still fresh in my mind. We'd even read an abstract of the old case in class, although my professor hadn't gone into much detail on it because it involved points of law that were deemed to be beyond the syllabus.

I found the law firm's template for PowerPoint presentations and put together a basic slide show. The presentation was only twenty minutes plus ten minutes for questions, so I stuck to ten slides with everything in large font.

I took the project seriously, but I didn't kid myself into believing that any of the partners would really care about what I had to say. They would be listening in to make sure I understood the core concepts and could talk about it without sounding like a nervous schoolgirl. Unfortunately, that's exactly what I was.

Public speaking terrified me. Any kind of presentation had me on edge. I would be nervous if friends asked me to stand up and tell them how my day had been. There was something about having people staring at me that I just couldn't come to grips with.

I liked to blend in with the crowd. In class, I would purposely avoid the front two rows, and try to find somewhere in the middle hoping that would help me blend in. It didn't work.

Most of my professors used the 'socratic method' of teaching. I'd never heard of it before starting law school, but apparently Socrates had liked to pick on nervous young girls and ask them to explain the ins and outs of the case we read before class.

No matter how well I knew the case, the words wouldn't come to me when I had to answer a question in front of all my peers. I usually ended up just quoting random sections from the case until the professor got bored and decided to move on to someone else.

The presentation was done with a day to spare, so I'd used the additional time to practice actually speaking it out loud. That was when I realized just how much Foster had screwed me over. This was obviously his way of getting back at me for the whole *pro bono* thing.

The presentation had been set aside for Friday afternoon, so my audience consisted of bored-looking associates, and partners who were all ready to head off to their beach houses in Delaware, or whatever else it was these people did on the weekends.

Foster showed up and sat at the front, because of course he would. This had all been his idea, and he damn well wasn't going to miss out on all the fun.

I'm going to kill him. Slowly.

184

I stood at the front of a large conference room while the partners talked to fellow colleagues that they hadn't seen in weeks, due to the tendency of most partners to lock themselves in their offices.

Most of the associates kept a respectful silence, but each of them had some form of caffeinated beverage in front of them, so the silence was likely as much due to exhaustion as anything else.

Foster coughed loudly, and after a few seconds the remaining conversation died down to a hush and finally there was total silence.

"Good evening, ladies and gentleman," I began. *God dammit, April. You're giving a presentation, not hosting the Oscars.* "I mean, good afternoon. I'll try not to keep you all here for too long today. As you may know, the Delaware Court of Chancery recently released a new decision on poison pills in takeovers. The court's reasoning in this case contains a few key differences from established case law that I want to draw to your attention."

I pressed a button on my laptop to change over the next slide which contained my bullet points summary the existing law.

"A lot of the current law on poison pills has been taken from the seminal case of…" I paused catching the smile spreading over Foster's face. "…the seminal case of Coch Industries."

My slide had shown the case as *In re Coch Ind. Shareholder Litigation*, but there was no getting around the fact that everyone in the legal profession just referred to the case as 'Coch,' or 'Coch Ind.'

There was no getting around the unfortunate pronunciation of the word 'Coch.' I made a point of saying the case name a lot at the beginning, hoping people would get used to hearing me say "Coch" again and again. Most of the attorneys in the room were well versed in the case, so they didn't react, but I did notice a few snickers from some of the attorneys working in non-corporate practice areas.

This was the easy bit. The next case was the real killer.

I turned on to the next slide and described how the Coch case had been used by courts in the last few years, and then flipped over the slide detailing the key points from the new case.

"Just last month, the Delaware SC released its judgment in the case of *In re Kunt, Inc. Shareholder Litigation.*"

Foster snickered loud enough for everyone in the room to hear, and he set off a few of the other attorneys as well. The partners didn't join in the laughing, and they had the decency to look vaguely embarrassed for me.

"The... the Kunt case will change the way we look at poison pills for companies without a diverse group of shareholders."

Instead of getting used to it, every time I said... the name of the case, the laughs grew louder and louder until I just gave up and started referring to it as 'the new case.'

The meeting room which, like the rest of the office, was usually too cold for comfort, now felt hot and suffocating. My blouse clung to the sweat pooling on my back, but I resisted the urge to stop and take off my cardigan. At least the cardigan covered the sweat patches.

The twenty minute presentation only lasted fifteen minutes, because I went through the rest of the material in a desperate panic. I'd be surprised if anyone could understand much of what I was saying, let alone follow the legal reasoning involved.

"Any questions?" I asked, adopting a tone of voice that I think made it very clear I didn't want any questions. My audience picked up on the hint.

All of them except one.

"Yes Foster. You have a question?" *Of course he has a fucking question.*

"I remember reading Coch in law school," Foster said. "It was a tricky case to get my head round, but from what I've heard, Kunt is really hard to understand. Do you agree that there are lots of complexities involved in understanding Kunt?"

I'm going to kill him. Slowly and painfully.

"Yes," I snarled. "It's a complicated case."

"But if you use Kunt correctly, you stand a good chance of getting a satisfactory outcome in your case?"

"I guess it depends which party you are," I replied. "I know some attorneys who think they understand the case, but actually they don't have a clue."

A few of the associates laughed, but Foster kept a straight face.

"If that's all--" I began.

"I have another question," Foster said. "If you were just getting started with corporate law, where would you recommend people start? Coch Ind. or Kunt?"

Foster spoke quickly and to my paranoid ears he managed to make "Ind. or" sound a lot like "in your."

I'm going to kill him. Slowly, painfully, and with a smile on my face.

"Coch," I replied, as I quickly shut my laptop and stormed out of the room.

He's going to pay for that. I headed straight back to my desk and opened up the motion that we'd prepared in Doris' case. We were still a long way from getting anywhere with finding her son, but we had to get the ball rolling.

It would take years, and I almost certainly wouldn't still be at the firm to see the end of it, but that was the way most things worked in the legal world. You had to wait years to see the results of your hard work. Presumably the wait was worth it in the end, but Doris might be dead by then.

Foster had asked for a draft of the motion ready for his final review over the weekend. Despite the huge fuss he'd made about not wanting to do *pro bono* work, he'd actually written most of the motion himself and I'd only chipped in on the statement of facts and some of the procedural sections.

The last thing I'd been working on was getting proper case citations in the document to conform to the court's standards. That sort of work always got dumped on the junior attorneys or summer associates, because we still had the citation rules fresh in our minds from law school.

Apart from a few more nuanced citations, I had basically finished the project and could send it over to Foster with only about thirty minutes more work.

Screw that.

If Foster liked rude case names, then that's exactly what he was going to get—a motion full of rude case names. He sucked at doing citations, so now he'd have to spend the entire weekend in the office with his Bluebook fixing it all. Served him right.

My mind might not be as filthy as Foster's, but I still knew enough dirty terms to litter the twelve pages with enough profanity and sexual innuendo to make a porn star blush.

Revenge was sweet.

Chapter Twenty-Seven

FOSTER

April was up to something. She had to be.

Ever since Friday's unfortunate presentation, I'd been keeping a keen eye on April to see how she would act around me. I prepared for a volley of verbal abuse, but instead she just stayed in her office hard at work.

I couldn't spend any time with her at the weekend, but that was probably for the best. Gave her time to cool off. I seemed to be doing that a lot lately. I should probably stop being such a jerk to her, but it takes time to change twenty-nine years of habit.

We finally met up on Monday, but instead of getting an earful from her she just smiled and spoke to me as if nothing had happened. She kept that up all week. I decided to test her resolve by inviting her to dinner on Friday night, but much to my amazement she agreed.

This out-of-character behavior made me suspicious, but other than making my own coffee and not eating any of the food she offered me, there didn't seem to be much I could do about it.

April had even stopped giving me grief about PorTupe, or at least, she didn't give me as much grief about it. She'd turned her attention instead to the *pro bono* case we were working on. I'd told April a hundred times that Doris' case wasn't going to go anywhere fast and that the motion would take time to be processed, but she still kept asking.

Just as I was about to head out for lunch, the phone rang from an undisclosed number. Unknown numbers had me on edge at the moment, because I was still waiting for another call from Zach. He'd been worryingly silent for too long, however this wasn't him.

"Foster Arrington," I said, as I answered the call.

"Hello Mr. Arrington, my name is Terrance Castle and I'm an intern for Judge Whiteman."

I knew that judge's name. Where did I know if from?

"How can I help you Mr. Castle?" I asked, as I typed 'Judge Whiteman' into the search bar on my emails. Bingo. He was the judge in Doris' case.

"I'm calling about the motion you filed recently with this court." He reeled off a document number, but we'd only made one filing so I didn't bother taking a note of it. "The judge would like a conference with you."

"Really?" I asked, not bothering to hide my surprise.

We'd requested that the case be expedited, but that meant we wanted to cut a few of the deadlines down from ninety days to thirty. We hadn't been expecting a conference with the judge.

"Yes," the clerk responded. "And he would like the conference to be tomorrow."

"Tomorrow!" If I'd had a drink in my mouth, I would have spat it out. "That's most unusual, Mr. Castle. Can you tell me what it's about? You're not exactly leaving me a lot of time to prepare."

"I can't say, Mr. Arrington, but as one professional to another, I would strongly recommend that you turn up. You're going to want to be there to speak to the judge."

"Uh, okay, sure."

I made a note of the time, and called April into my office. I didn't make that many court appearances, but I worked with plenty of attorneys who did. I knew that you rarely just showed up to court on less than twenty-four hours notice for a meeting with a judge. Other than refamiliarizing myself with the facts of the case and the motion we'd submitted, there wasn't a lot we could do to prepare.

"You rang, m'lord," April said, showing up in my doorway and giving a sarcastic curtsy. I wouldn't mind lifting that skirt up a little higher and having her call me sir, but right now work had to take precedence. *Although, we could sneak in a few hours... no, not now. Think about Zach. That's it.*

"I just got a call from the judge in Doris' case," I explained. "He wants us to go to the courtroom tomorrow for a meeting. And before you ask, no, I don't know what it's about. It's highly unusual to have a meeting at such short notice."

"I suppose he just wants to talk about our motion," April replied. "That's a good thing isn't it."

"Maybe. You should come along as well. It'll be a great experience for you, especially if you keep insisting on protecting the small fry instead of the big fish with money. You'll be spending a lot of time in court if that's the case."

"There's nothing wrong with fighting for people's rights in court."

"I meant, you'll be in court fighting to enforce judgments so that you get paid by all your broke ass clients. We should spend some time going over the motion before tomorrow. It's been weeks since I looked at it, so you know the facts better than me."

April's face turned a shade of pale I had never seen before. She hadn't even looked that white when she'd found out our parents had got married.

"You feeling okay?" I asked. "If you're going to throw up would you perhaps mind going to the bathroom?"

"You haven't read the brief in weeks?" April asked.

"No, why?"

"But you submitted it to the court?"

"Yes. I had my paralegal do it on Monday."

"So you didn't check my citations?"

"God no," I replied dismissively. "I haven't done that since law school. I have complete confidence in your abilities to properly cite everything. You don't need me to check that."

Just when I thought April couldn't get any paler, she somehow found another shade of white I didn't know existed.

"I may know why we've been called in to see the judge," April said softly. She bit her lip and tried to smile, but it came out as more of a constipated grimace. "You're going to laugh when you hear this."

-*-

"Is that your special 'court suit?' " April asked when we met outside the courtroom.

I often wore a suit to work, but the jacket would quickly get thrown over the chair and not worn again until it was time to leave. I rarely wore a tie. Couldn't stand the things.

"This is my 'I'm going to get torn a new one by the judge suit.' I only wear it on the rare occasions when a summer associate thinks it's funny to put a load of silly case names into a court document."

"You should have checked it before filing it," April insisted.

She'd apologized profusely yesterday, but as time passed she'd clearly decided that perhaps this wasn't entirely her fault after all. I should have checked the document, especially after I'd just put April through hell with that presentation.

"What sort of stuff did you put in there anyway?" I asked.

"Bad stuff," she replied. "Naughty things."

"Hmm, well, in that case I can't be too mad I suppose. You look nervous."

"I'm terrified. My heart's racing a mile a minute. Aren't you worried?"

"I always try to remain calm. My heart rate only goes up during exercise and certain other physical activities. Look." I took her hand and pressed it against my chest so that she could feel my heart.

"That's strangely therapeutic. I think it's actually helping me calm down."

She kept her hand on my chest until the large wooden door opened and a man in his early twenties, presumably the court clerk, told us to come inside.

The judge was sitting in his chair, which meant this was going to be an official reaming. I told April to sit in one of the seats at the side while I went up and approached the bench.

April had insisted on coming along and owning up to the whole thing, but I'd made it clear she was to keep quiet. The last thing I wanted was to make this look like I was throwing my summer associate under the bus.

"You might as well both come up here," the judge said, in a deep booming voice. "I'm guessing the young lady had something to do with this as well."

"No your honor, it was all me," I replied, motioning with my hand for April to stay seated.

"Really? So you cited a Supreme Court case as being between the parties of 'My Tight Pussy' versus 'Your Hard Cock.'"

"Um…"

"And," the judge continued, "while I respect the privacy of what two consenting adults get up to in the bedroom, I can't help but think that you did not write 'the court held that you must pull my long blonde hair the next time you take me from behind.'"

With pleasure, April.

I turned around and saw her desperately looking everywhere other than at the judge. There wasn't much I could do to keep her out of it now, so I motioned for her to come and join me.

"Obviously, your honor, that motion should never have been filed. It was intended as a joke. I just filed the wrong one."

"Clearly. Look, I don't care what goes on between you two. You wouldn't be the first pair of lawyers to have an office romance--I can vouch for that personally--however when you took on this case you accepted a significant responsibility."

"Yes, your honor," I said, with April repeating it after me. "Obviously I accept full responsibility for this. It won't happen again."

"No, it had better not. I do hope you intend to take your *pro bono* responsibilities seriously from now on, Mr. Arrington?"

"Certainly, your honor."

"You could prove that by, for example, volunteering at the the local law school to help with the moot court competition. I'm sure two intelligent young attorneys like yourselves could find a way to help."

"That sounds like an excellent suggestion," I said reluctantly, as a weekend spent screwing April disappeared before my eyes.

"Good. If that's the case, I don't see any need for further disciplinary action. Have fun, you two."

The judge banged his gavel, and strolled off whistling and clearly feeling rather pleased with his morning's work.

"What just happened?" April asked as we left the courtroom.

"You landed us with a weekend spent listening to law students give crappy oral arguments. That's what happened."

"Oh. Well, it could be worse."

"If you say so. I hate law students."

"Thanks. No offense taken."

"You're the exception. Now, let's go back to the office and read over this motion you wrote. I have a feeling this one is going to be a lot less dry than usual."

Chapter Twenty-Eight

APRIL

I considered myself a studious person, but you had to be a special kind of insane to be at law school on a Saturday during the summer break.

Even so, people were huddled over books in all the common areas, and no doubt the library would still be half-full. I may not have much of a life myself, but I could console myself in thinking that perhaps there were people with even less of a social presence.

Foster had arrived at the school early and arranged for us to both be judges, despite the fact that I would have less moot court experience than the contestants. All I'd done was compete in the mandatory first-year competition, and even though I'd enjoyed it, I'd not signed up for any more competitions. Court appearances were rare for corporate work, so it had seemed like a waste of my energy. Now, I wished I knew what was going on so as not to look completely stupid.

Mind you, it's not like Foster had all that much experience either. He'd bragged about winning one of the moot court competitions while he'd been in law school, but when I'd questioned him about it, he'd admitted to having slept with both of the female judges. Knowing what he was like in bed, they were bound to have voted in his favor.

"How did you get us on the judging panel?" I asked Foster. "I'm still a law student. Some of the other judges are actual judges."

"Judge Whiteman was supposed to be on the panel. He had to pull out which is no doubt why he conveniently suggested we show up here today."

"He screwed us over, didn't he?"

"Completely," Foster agreed. "Come on, let's go take our seats."

We strolled into one of the law school's moot court rooms, and sat on the raised table that looked down on the lawyers' podiums. I'd stood on one of those podiums just over a year ago. It was terrifying down there looking up at the judges.

I couldn't imagine anyone being particularly scared looking up at me, but I had to admit, I definitely felt more powerful in this position. I suppose there had to be some advantages to being a judge; it certainly had nothing to do with the meager pay.

I didn't recognize any of the names on the list of contestants, so at least I wouldn't be judging any of the few friends I had at law school.

The first two contestants stood up at the podium and introduced themselves to Foster, myself, and the third judge. The first speaker, a nervous guy who started sweating within minutes, gave his prepared speech about why his client's position on some contract issue was the correct one and that the court should decide in his favor to avoid an unconscionable outcome.

He alternated eye contact between all three judges, as I knew he had been told to do, and I tried to look reassuring, but he didn't grow in confidence. The third judge asked most of the questions, but Foster chipped in with a few as well. I intended to remain quiet unless something caught my attention. It was harder to sound stupid when you didn't say anything.

By the time we listened to the same arguments for the fourth time, my eyes had glazed over and only the third judge had retained any kind of interest in proceedings.

Foster scribbled something on his pad of paper and pushed it towards me. *Do you know of anywhere we can go to get some privacy?*

The man had a one-track mind. Fortunately, I liked the direction that track was taking.

Lecture halls on top floor are usually quiet, I wrote on my paper. *Why? :-)*

I need to take a nap.

Not what I'd been expecting.

I went to write a response, when Foster's hand grabbed hold of my thigh and gave it a firm squeeze. Immediately all the nerves and tension I'd felt pretending to be a judge evaporated, and a warmth flooded my body, relaxing every muscle and making it almost impossible to keep my eyes open.

His fingers crept up my leg, turning the warmth to a fire, which started igniting my senses. I fought to keep my eyes open, but all I wanted to do was close them and throw my head back while Foster teased me to the point of ecstasy.

The girl kept giving me funny looks and I could swear she knew what was going on. I snapped out of my trance and tried to peel Foster's hand off my thigh. I might as well have tried to remove my own foot from my leg. His hand was wedged on tight, as if it were a part of my body.

I gave up, but then Foster decided to remove his hand anyway. Typical. When I wanted him to do something, he fought me, even if that's what he wanted to do regardless. He was such a stubborn ass sometimes.

No sooner was his hand off my thigh, than he had taken hold of my hand and placed it right between his legs. I couldn't fight him. If I struggled in any way then it would be obvious what was happening under the table, if it wasn't already.

Foster's cock was rock hard already. My fingers curled around the thick shaft and squeezed tightly enough that I could feel blood pulsing through the thick vein running up the middle. Just thinking about Foster's meat pumping into me had me dripping wet between my legs. My body acted on impulse around him, and I was hopeless to exert any kind of control.

I tried stroking his cock, but his pants and belt got in the way, so I had to give up. I wrote another note on the paper. *I hope that erection isn't because you were looking at her.* I didn't know the name of the law student currently speaking in front of us, but she was undeniably pretty and her top opened enough at the front to tease the large breasts that lay underneath. Even I'd looked twice.

It's all for you, came the reply.

After the fourth presentation, we'd finally earned ourselves an hour break for lunch. Foster quickly made it clear he had no intention of joining the third judge and the contestants for the free lunch provided in one of the communal rooms.

"Come on," he said, grabbing my hand and leading me towards the stairs. "I hear there's a lecture room on the top floor that should be vacant."

I needed to start working out more, because by the time we made it to the fourth floor I was out of breath and breathing heavily just trying to keep up with Foster who practically sprinted to the top.

Sure enough, the lecture room on the top floor was completely empty. A feeling of dread washed over me as I walked inside; I associated this room with Civil

Procedure classes, and that would put a damper on anyone's sexual desire. Not for long though.

"Where do you sit?" Foster asked.

I pointed him to an aisle seat about halfway down. It was the perfect spot, almost exactly in the middle of the room, allowing me to blend in with the crowd and not get noticed.

Foster took off his suit jacket, yanked off his tie, and brazenly unbuttoned his shirt, before sitting down in my seat. The middle of his shirt hung tantalizingly open, revealing part of his firm pecs and most of his solid abs.

"Someone could walk in at any minute," I said nervously, looking around to double check that the room was empty.

"No one's going to walk in."

"What if they do?"

"Then they see us having fun. Who cares? If you don't start undressing right this second, I'm going to do my shirt back up and I know you don't want that."

He was right. I didn't.

I slipped off my blazer and tugged my blouse out of my skirt. It's about time I had some fun in here.

Chapter Twenty-Nine

APRIL

I'd never stripped for a man before. Not like this.

Usually the clothes just sort of came off in a blur and I didn't have to think about it much. This was very different.

I stood just five feet from Foster and slowly undressed, feeling like a stripper as his eyes moved over my body, taking in every inch of me on display. Perhaps the comparison should have been to a porn star auditioning for a movie; strippers probably didn't do what I was about to do to Foster.

I reached behind me and pulled down the zipper on my skirt, before letting it drop to the floor. The blouse quickly followed. Thank God I'd started wearing nicer underwear. The bra and panties even matched; it almost looked like I'd prepared for this. Maybe subconsciously I had.

Foster's eyes came back up to meet mine. I shivered even though the room wasn't cold.

"You look stunning," Foster remarked sincerely.

I felt stunning. Not in the traditional sense, mind you. But it was impossible not to feel sexy when someone like Foster was looking at you the way he was looking at me right now. He was using all his willpower to stay seated and not come over and ravage me. There'd be plenty of time for that.

I stepped out of the dress, but kept my high heels on. They might not be practical, but the additional height helped me feel a little more powerful, and that's what I wanted right now; to be in charge.

I walked towards Foster, but he held up a hand to stop me. "All of it," he said, motioning for me to get completely naked.

"Not yet," I replied. "You don't get to give the orders today."

Foster frowned, but then quickly raised his eyebrows as I dropped to my knees in front of him. His hands instinctively grabbed hold of the back of my head, but I shook them off. I was setting the pace now.

My hand reached out slowly and hesitantly towards the bulge in his pants, as if I were about to touch something that might scald me.

I grasped his cock and gave it a teasing squeeze before slowly pulling down the zipper and reaching inside to put my flesh on his. His cock was too hard and too large to get it through his boxers and pants, so I yanked both of them down until I was face-to-cock with Foster's beast.

My fingers closed around the warm flesh as I slowly stroked the shaft, examining it with my eyes as if I'd never seen one before. I suppose in some ways I hadn't. Certainly none of my ex-boyfriends had come this well-equipped.

I looked up at Foster and licked my lips before moving my head slowly towards his tip. When my tongue was close enough to reach out and lick the salty fluid appearing on top, I stopped and stared back up at him with a seductive smile.

"You're not going to make me beg, are you?" Foster asked. "'Cause I'll do it. I'll do whatever it takes to get those perfect, pert lips clamped around my cock."

His cock pulsed in my hand, getting quicker and quicker as the urgency built within it. He might explode with just me knelt in front of him stroking his cock.

I kept looking up at Foster, as my tongue darted out and licked up the precum from his tip. As soon as I'd had a taste of the salty goodness, I knew I wouldn't be able to hold out any longer. I wanted to taste him.

My tongue moved around the the bottom of the head, as I flicked my tongue lightly against the sensitive skin of his tip. Foster let out a loud moan of encouragement, but the pulsing of his cock in my hand was all the indication I needed to know he was enjoying it.

I locked my lips around his head, and let my tongue circle the very end of his cock, until finally I sucked hard and let go with a loud 'pop.'

I knew I wouldn't be able to take all of him in my mouth, but I wanted to give it a damn good try. I let go of the shaft and placed both hands on his thighs before lowering my mouth down onto his cock.

Foster's hands kept flinching and I knew he was fighting the desire to grab hold of my head and fuck my mouth. I enjoyed knowing I could tease him as much as he could tease me.

I made it halfway down before coming back up for air, but I knew I could take more. I just had to fight the gag reflex. I sucked hard as I came up, slurping on him with little regard for being ladylike, and inhaled loudly as I released.

"Holy shit, baby," Foster groaned. "Keep doing exactly that."

Each time my lips slid down his cock--coated in my saliva--I took a little bit more of him inside me until his tip tickled the back of my throat. Taking three quarters of a cock that size *had* to be considered an achievement.

Foster was close. His quads had tensed so firmly that I expected him to cramp up at any moment, and so much blood had flowed to his head I finally understood why some men referred to it as a 'purple-headed warrior.'

I desperately wanted to taste him, but there was no way I could go back downstairs without having his cock inside me. I'd feel empty and unused.

I stood up, leaving Foster gasping and on the edge of exploding.

"Come here," he moaned. "I want to taste that pussy."

"No," I replied. I reached behind my back and unhooked my bra, before sliding it off my shoulders and letting it join my blouse and dress on the floor. I turned around and slowly pulled down my panties, bending over as I did so to reveal my slick wet pussy which desperately need him inside.

I heard Foster gasp and quickly undress. In the space of only ten seconds he had gotten naked and slipped a condom over his cock. I knew that likely came from practice, but right now that didn't bother me.

He stood up, but I pushed him back down again.

"How many times do I have to tell you, I'm in control right now."

"Yes, ma'am," Foster replied sitting back down on the seat and facing the aisle.

I straddled his thighs, and looked him dead in the eyes as I slowly lowered my ass to his cock. I reached a hand behind me to guide his cock between my folds. Once his tip was inside me, I dropped myself down and let him fill me up, moaning loudly as I did so.

I did my best to look serious and domineering, as I aggressively rocked my hips on his cock, however there was nothing I could do to stop myself groaning loudly each time my clit rubbed against his pubic mound.

Foster's hands gripped my ass cheeks to help me keep up the pace while I rested my arms on his shoulders. His fingers moved around my crack, occasionally teasing my asshole, threatening to enter, but never quite doing it.

The thrill of the unexpected had me coming in a few short minutes. I thrust my hips hard against his stomach and held my clit against him as I came silently, the only noise being the final gasps of air forced out of my lungs, and the quivering of my spent muscles as they tried to remain balanced on Foster's thighs.

I was so utterly exhausted, I almost completely forgot that Foster was still rock hard inside of me. I remembered what I wanted--needed--more than anything, and quickly clambered off his lap and dropped back down to my knees.

Foster threw the condom to one side, as I sucked him again. This time I let him hold my head down on his cock as he growled loudly--his body vibrating with the intensity of his passion--and emptied himself inside my mouth.

I quickly swallowed everything he had to give me, gulping the hot, salty liquid down like it was water and I was stranded in the desert.

After I'd drank every last drop, Foster pulled me to my feet and stood in front of me, before placing a finger under my chin and pulling me in for a kiss. The kiss started off soft and gentle, but soon became more intense as if we were kissing before the sex, not after it.

Finally, we broke apart and Foster placed his hands on my hips, pulling me in towards him.

"I feel guilty," he said. "I never did anything for you."

"I got mine," I replied, with a satisfied smile. I quickly got dressed and watched Foster do the same, his tattooed, and muscular chest disappearing under the formal white shirt and tie. "However," I continued, "don't talk so much this afternoon. I plan to put your tongue to work later."

"I'm going to eat you for hours," he replied. I believed him.

I left Foster staring at my ass as I walked up the stairs, making sure to put a lot more wiggle in it than usual.

It wasn't until I saw Foster again in the moot court room that I realized the impact of what I'd said. I was as good as admitting that we were going to fuck again. We weren't just people who did it on the spur of the moment because they couldn't control themselves. We were a couple.

Shit had just gotten real.

Chapter Thirty

FOSTER

I think I'm in a relationship.

At the very least I'm dating someone. That's... unusual.

I also appear to be happy about it.

April spent Saturday night and all of Sunday at my apartment, and to say we didn't get a lot of sleep would be a huge fucking understatement.

It wasn't the first time I'd gone into work on Monday morning looking a little worse for wear, so I had a way to minimize the damage. Most people made a complete hash of it. They would come in late and still look exhausted. Everyone would see them show up, and before you knew it word had got around the office that the person was tired, hungover, or just still drunk.

My way avoided most of those problems. First of all, I would arrive at work extra early. Hell, when you'd had as little sleep as me, a few extra hours won't make any difference. Coming in early meant no one saw you until you'd had a few cups of coffee. I would then usually sneak out early for the day and bill the last few hours from home in bed.

I probably should have told April about my approach.

She walked into work looking like she hadn't slept in forty-eight hours. Wearing her sunglasses all the way until she arrived at her office, just made it even more obvious. *Schoolgirl error, April.*

Everyone noticed she looked tired, and I heard a few people comment, but people still felt sorry for her after the presentation so she had earned a little bit of leeway.

I'd given the instruction for my secretary to intercept all my calls, but anyone who had my direct number could get straight through. I made it until ten o'clock when the phone rang, the ringtone snapping me awake as I'd been drifting off to sleep at my desk.

In my disorientation, I answered the call immediately without checking who it was. My blurry vision finally focused on the name on the caller ID screen, but it was too late. Zach.

"How's my favorite referral source doing this morning?" Zach asked cheerfully.

I sighed and rubbed my eyes. I was far too tired for this shit.

"I've never referred a client to you, Zach, and I don't intend to start now. Did you want something? Or are you just bored waiting for Daddy to provide you some more coloring books to fill in while you pretend to be a lawyer."

"Very good," Zach replied sarcastically. Sarcasm, the lowest form of wit. Unless I was the one doing it, in which case it was dry and clever. "I've done some digging around. I'm right about April."

"Are you going to tell me how she's doomed and is never going to work as a lawyer again?"

"That's about the gist of it."

"And I suppose, like last time, you're not actually going to tell me what the hell you're talking about."

"Oh, I'll tell you," Zach said. "But you might not want to hear it."

"Just tell me so I can get on with grown-up work."

"If you insist. Turns out April has committed a pretty serious breach of ethics."

Did he know about the naughty motion we filed in Doris' case? No, this whole thing started before that was filed. Besides, we'd cleared that up.

"It's not a breach of ethics to refuse to sleep with a slimy associate. Goodbye Zach."

"Wait," he said quickly. Whatever it was he had to say, he really wanted to say it this time. "Okay, you want the details? Fine. April has worked both sides of the same case. You guys must have fucked up the conflict check, because I know for a fact she worked for Jacob Oscar on the shareholder vote issue."

"There was no conflict," I said calmly. I'd run the conflict check personally like I always did. "She's never represented the shareholders."

"That's where you're wrong," Zach said. "She worked on that exact same issue while she was at Cooper & Cooper. I helped her with it. We represent the shareholders."

If that was true… shit. It wasn't worth thinking about. Except in extreme circumstances, working for both parties in the same case was almost impossible, and you would always have to get written consent from everyone concerned. We sure as hell hadn't done that.

But it couldn't be true. I'd run the fucking conflict check.

"You're lying," I said firmly. "I know you must be bored over there, but you really need to think of a better way to spend your time than trying to ruin someone's career before they've even been admitted to the bar."

"She never will be admitted to the bar once this gets out. I'll give you a few hours to check the facts. Meet me outside our office building at one o'clock today. We can start discussing how you're going to handover PorTupe to me."

"Goodbye Zach."

This time I hung up the phone before he had a chance to respond. Zach always sounded sure of himself, but there was an extra bit of certainty in his voice today. He'd done some fact-checking and still thought April had done something wrong. That didn't bode well.

I ran the conflict check again, running the names of the shareholders in the suit against Jacob's company. Nothing came up.

I searched the system and found the spreadsheet that April had prepared and sent off to the risk management advisor at the firm. I scrolled through the list, but couldn't see anything wrong. I'd nearly made it to the bottom when I spotted the error.

Oh fuck. Oh fuck, oh fuck, oh fuck.

April had made two mistakes on the conflict list. Combined, those mistakes had let the conflict slip through unnoticed. Cooper & Cooper represented the shareholders who had filed suit against Jacob's company, and it looked like Zach was right. April had worked on that case, however instead of listing all the shareholder names she had only listed the first shareholder who appeared on the court filings. And she'd spelt it wrong.

This was bad. Really fucking bad. The case could get thrown out and we wouldn't be paid. I had no clue what would happen to April, but at the very least she'd have to go through some extra steps before being admitted to the bar. At worst... well, Zach might be right on that point.

I quickly edited April's spreadsheet to show the correct client name and then typed in all the other shareholders for good measure. I made the same changes in the firm's conflict of interest database. That should help cover April's ass at least.

April should have noticed that she'd worked on this case before, but as a summer associate she'd probably been given only a small segment of the case to work on. She may not have even known the name of the other party. That would help her defense, but I'd rather we never got to that stage. That meant talking to Zach.

If he thought I was going to give up my best client then he had another thing coming.

Chapter Thirty-One

FOSTER

I strolled out of the office with my sleeves rolled up to reveal my tattoos. I rarely walked around in public with them on display because they didn't exactly scream "reputable lawyer," but right now that wasn't the image I wanted to give out.

Zach stood there outside his office building waiting for me. He saw me approach and motioned for us to head in the direction of a nearby park. That was fine with me. I'd feel less inclined to hold back if we had a bit of privacy.

We ended up under the shade of a tree, which did little to help keep me cool in the suffocating humidity. I'd been in D.C. for over five years now, but I still wasn't used to the constant feeling of being in a greenhouse when outdoors.

The summer months were torture, but even in the winter you would get a humid day spring up out of nowhere, making you sweaty and sticky under a thick coat.

I'd been struggling to control my temper while I was indoors; outdoors in this heat, it was almost impossible.

"I'm going to assume you found out that I'm right," Zach said. "About April committing a big no-no. Otherwise you wouldn't be here."

"Perhaps I'm just here to punch your lights out," I replied. "Or did that not occur to you? At least there's nothing for you to fall over here."

"Very droll. It still amazes me that someone like you," he paused to look down at my tattoos, "managed to become a lawyer. You were bound to fuck up eventually, it's just a shame you had to drag someone like April down with you."

"It's not her fault," I said. "I'm the one to blame. I messed up the conflict check."

"Oh, I know. I always suspected as much. April's far too perfect to make such a basic mistake. Fucking little Princess."

"Watch your fucking mouth," I snapped. "You are in no position to be insulting anyone's character, least of all hers."

"Whatever. The fact is, all I have to do is send out an email and within hours shit will hit the fan, so to speak. I'm guessing your firm will fire April immediately, and you will likely be placed on leave. Then there's the disciplinary hearings. Oh, they're going to be so much fun. I might go along for shits and giggles."

"You're not going to send those emails."

"I hope you're right," Zach said, trying to sound sincere. "I don't want to send them. You know what I want."

"You're not getting my biggest client."

"You can hardly work for them if you're suspended. You really have no choice in all this."

"We can go back to the bit where I knock you the fuck out," I said threateningly.

"I've got you over a barrel, Foster," Zach said, before laughing loudly to himself. "I know you're dumb, but you're not that dumb. In fact, I reckon I could take a swing at you right now and you wouldn't even react."

"Go on then," I said, as I moved within punching distance of Zach.

He looked around to make sure no one was looking and to my immense surprise he swung a punch. To my even greater surprise, he managed to make contact.

I let my head swing to the right as his fist collided with the left side of my face. My tongue checked for damaged teeth, but found none.

I pretended to barely feel the punch, but the truth was that even the weakest, most feeble punch to the face did hurt at least a bit.

Fortunately it also hurt the person doing the punching. Zach smiled, but I could see him wincing in pain, and trying to hide the discomfort in his right hand. He'd probably never punched anyone before, not unless it had been part of some silly frat boy dare.

This would usually be the part where I swung a punch of my own and sent Zach to the floor in a crying heap. This time I'd be sure to break some bones in the process; he deserved it.

But I couldn't punch him and we both knew it.

"Does that make you feel better?" I asked. I could taste some blood in my mouth, but I swallowed it so as not to give him the pleasure of knowing he'd actually made me bleed.

"Yes, it does. Not as good as it's going to feel when I get promoted after bringing in such a huge new client though. I probably won't make partner immediately, but I'm going to jump a few levels without a doubt."

"You know, there's more to being a lawyer than bringing in clients," I pointed out. "You actually have to do the work as well. Or would you like me to do that for you too?"

"If you insist on making this difficult, then I might just have to do that. Now then, shall we talk business. I want that client on my books within the next two months. That gives you a month to start severing ties, and a month to find a way to introduce me with a glowing reference."

"I'm not doing it," I replied.

"Yes, you are," Zach yelled. He was like a spoiled child, used to getting everything his own way and never being told 'no.' "I'm not bluffing, Foster. I *will* do it."

"Go ahead then. I don't care. PorTupe is worth a lot more to me than Jacob's current case, and I'm confident I'll stay out of trouble. Mistakes happen."

"And what about April?" Zach asked. "Are you just going to hang her out to dry?"

I tried to effect a casual shrug, but I still hadn't gotten the hang of it. I'd have to practice in front of the mirror one day.

"I don't care what happens to a summer associate," I lied. "She made her bed. She'll have to lie in it."

"She will. Alone no doubt. That frigid bitch is soon going to find out what the real world's like."

"What did you just call her?" I snarled.

Zach hesitated, as if his brain was trying to impart important information, like how it might not be a good idea to answer that question.

"It's true," Zach said. "None of the guys in the office got anywhere with her. Not even me. Like I said, she's a frigid bitch."

This time I definitely broke some bones. Or perhaps it was a tooth chipping off in his mouth. Either way, the punch landed hard on the side of his face.

Zach went sprawling against the tree which kept him up on his feet and gave me the chance to swing another blow, this time higher up. He'd have a real shiner of a black eye in a few hours.

He collapsed on the floor and curled up in a fetal position. I drew back a foot to kick him in the stomach, but I couldn't bring myself to kick such a feeble, helpless creature when it was curled up on the floor. I liked to punch people face-to-face, so I could look them in the eye as I did it.

A few people had seen me punch him and small crowds were starting to gather. The general public tended to act on instinct and what they saw was two men in suits arguing. For most people, that didn't constitute anything they needed to get involved in.

I walked straight back to the office and soaked my knuckles under cold water. The harder you punched, the harder it hurt afterwards. The adrenaline kept most of the pain away, but they'd still sting for the rest of the day.

I'd fucked up. Any chance I'd had of stopping Zach from reporting April and me to the state bar had just gone out the window. In truth, me punching him probably hadn't made a difference. I'd made my choice.

I'd decided to keep PorTupe, even though I was starting to intensely dislike the directors the more April told me about them. I'd brushed off her complaints, but they left a nasty taste in the mouth. I didn't like working for people like that, but it was too late now.

I could handle a suspension and a slap on the wrist. April might not be so lucky.

Chapter Thirty-Two

APRIL

Your boyfriend chose money over your career. You're fucked.

Zach had been taunting me all morning with a series of texts, that I'd tried my best to ignore until that last one. Apparently he had evidence that I'd committed a major breach of legal ethics, but I had no idea what he was talking about.

His final message made it clear that Foster had refused to play ball, and now I was in serious trouble. As if to confirm that, an email popped up from Kathleen demanding that I go to her office immediately.

We'd agreed not to act as stepmother and stepdaughter at work, and judging by the tone of this email, Kathleen had no issues sticking to her side of the bargain on that one.

I took the long walk over to Kathleen's corner office situated on the floor above mine. I'd only ever been on this floor once before and that was to use the bathroom when ours had been shut for cleaning.

Unlike her son, Kathleen kept her door open and she beckoned me inside when she saw me approach.

"Shut the door behind you," she said sternly. Yeah, this wasn't going to be a fun meeting. "Do you know why I've called you in here today?"

"No," I replied. That was sort of true. I still didn't understand what the hell was going on, other than Zach's cryptic messages.

"This isn't easy for me to say, April, but I'm going to have to let you go."

Whoa, this just got real serious, real quick.

"What? Why?"

I only had a few more weeks left, and I'd earned more than enough money to get me through the final year of law school, but the bigger problem was trying to find another job for after graduation.

I'd now been fired by two law firms and I hadn't even finished law school. What the hell was wrong with me?

"We've received a very serious allegation that you worked for the other side in the Jacob Oscar matter last year at Cooper & Cooper. As I'm sure you know, that is a serious breach of the ABA's ethics rules, and means you may have breached client confidences."

"Of course," I muttered, "but I don't even know who the other party is in Jacob's case. Foster never gave me the details."

I had worked on a similar legal area at Cooper & Cooper, which was why I'd been able to produce a decent memo for Jacob. I suppose the facts had been similar, but Foster had never given me any of the opposition parties' names.

"Do any of these names ring a bell? Mendleson Co., NormArtTech, N. Gaige…"

"Yes," I said, as my heart started pounding in my chest. "Yes, I worked for those clients, but I put them on my conflict list. I'm sure I did."

How could this have happened? Arrington & Hedges had draconian internal policies and procedures to catch this kind of thing. I'd prepared the conflict checklist exactly as directed.

"You did," Kathleen said. "Foster ran a conflict check, but he must have fucked it up." Kathleen rubbed her temples with her fingers, and sighed loudly. "I'm sorry April, this is not entirely your fault, but you have to live with the consequences. You still should have spotted the overlap and raised a red flag, but it's Foster's fault as well. When he sees the sight of money and billable hours, he gets reckless and plows ahead without thinking things through."

She didn't need to explain that to me. I'd seen first hand how Foster always put money before everything else. I thought I meant more to him than that. Apparently not. He'd had a chance to fix this, but that would have meant losing out financially. That was a step he wasn't prepared to take. Not for me.

"So what happens now?" I asked.

"I'm going to do what I can to fix this," Kathleen explained. "But I still have to let you go. We can't risk it looking like you're providing us with information on your former client."

"I understand."

"I wish I did. It sounds like you made a real enemy over at Cooper & Cooper. How does someone as nice as you manage that?"

"By rejecting his advances," I replied.

Not to mention the fact that Foster punched him. If Foster had never showed up that night, this would probably never have happened. I would be at Cooper & Cooper now, and Foster would just be a normal

223

stepbrother, albeit one that I would look at inappropriately whenever I saw him.

"I see. Well, like I said, I'm going to do what I can, but you'll need to pack up your things and leave."

I nodded and quickly got up and left. I only just made it back to my office before I started to cry. Foster had given me some incredible moments over the last nine months, but he'd also destroyed my life and had gotten me fired from two jobs.

How could he have messed up something so simple as a conflict check? It occurred to me that perhaps Kathleen had been lying. Foster had probably never even run the check at all. Maybe he'd asked his assistant to do it. Foster might as well have "Time is Money" printed somewhere on his chest, so it made sense that he would palm off all non-billable work to his assistant.

My login privileges hadn't been revoked yet, so I pulled up Jacob's client file on the system. Each client had an admin folder where things like engagement letters and conflict checks were stored.

There was nothing there. Foster hadn't even bothered to run the conflict check. I pulled up the conflict spreadsheet I had prepared on my first day, and sure enough, the names of all the opposing parties in the Jacob case were there in black and white. If he'd run the check I wouldn't have lost my job.

At least his office was empty right now. I didn't want to give him the satisfaction of seeing me leave. I shoved the photos of Mom and Dad into my bag, and looked around my office one final time.

Apparently fate didn't want me to be a lawyer. Nor did it want me to be in a happy relationship. I just wish fate had passed on the message before I'd wasted two years at law school and fallen hard for Foster.

At least now I knew the real man underneath the suit. Underneath the tattoos. Underneath the thick muscles that covered his body. Foster wanted money and success. He would happily fuck me in his spare time, but the second I got in the way of his primary goal, he would throw me to one side without a moment's thought.

I went back to my apartment and filled out the paperwork to withdraw from law school. I didn't have to pay tuition, but I was still going into debt for living expenses and casebooks at $200 per subject. There didn't seem much point it finishing if I was never going to be a lawyer anyway.

Dad had said Mom would be proud of me no matter what I did, but I doubted that included quitting. Mom had her flaws, but she never quit.

Sorry Mom. I just can't do this.

Chapter Thirty-Three

FOSTER

I should have thought this through. Why did I always have to act on instinct?

Zach called my bluff. He went through with it. April had been fired and she wouldn't return my calls.

Zach had been right; I was an idiot. No matter how good I was as a lawyer, I still couldn't control my base emotions. I'd reacted with my fists and now everything good in my life had disappeared in an instant.

I went to April's apartment, but she didn't answer the door. I knew where she would go when times were hard, so I hopped on a flight and went back to New York.

She wasn't there either. Unfortunately my Mom was.

"I want a word with you," Mom yelled as I tried to sneak up to my room. I felt like a teenager sneaking back into the house after a night of drinking. I'd never been good at being subtle.

"What about?" I asked grumpily.

"You know what about. Are you going to explain what the hell happened with this Jacob situation?"

"We've already had this conversation. I fucked up, that's what happened. I forgot to run a conflict check."

"Don't give me that crap. I know when you're lying to me. I always have. I checked the conflict log on the database. You did run that conflict check."

"There's no conflict check on the system," I replied. "I checked."

"That's because you deleted it. I'm the managing partner, Foster, I have ways of finding these things out. You ran the conflict check and it came back negative. How did that happen?"

"Don't you have ways of finding that out?" I asked sarcastically.

"I'm giving you a chance to explain, Foster. A chance to tell me what the hell is going on here."

What's going on is that I've completely fucked everything up.

I didn't even care about the fallout for me. I was going to get shit for this, and I'd almost certainly end up with a black mark on my record, but worst of all, I'd lost April.

She'd done nothing wrong in all this. It wasn't her fault that some low-life took an interest in her and made her life hell. Then I came along, and my attempts to make things better had the complete opposite effect.

"Fine," I said, exasperated. I just want to get this conversation over with. "I deleted the file."

"That doesn't explain how the conflict check came back negative."

"April made a typo in the name, and she forgot to include the complete list of all parties. I changed the spreadsheet to hide her mistakes."

"I figured as much," Mom said. She didn't look the least bit surprised. "It doesn't take a genius to figure out why."

I let that comment slip by without response. I didn't have the energy for it right now. "What's going to happen now? Is there any way we can salvage this?"

"I already have," Mom said. I raised my eyebrows in surprise. "I'm not just a pretty face you know, Foster. I have connections. Connections at Cooper & Cooper."

"You'll never convince Zach to drop this. He's fucking evil and he has a grudge against April. And against me as well. I may have accidentally broken his jaw."

"Accidentally?" Now it was Mom's turn to raise an eyebrow quizzically.

"Long story."

"It doesn't matter. I've had words with his father, and they're going to keep this information to themselves. Zach hadn't gotten around to making a formal complaint and he's not going to."

"How on Earth did you swing that?" I asked. Mom had achieved a lot in her career, but this was truly impressive.

"Let's just say I have information on what the father gets up to without his wife's knowledge."

"Oh Mom, please don't tell me you and him--"

"God no," she snapped. "Give me some credit. But I know some of the women *and men* that he's had affairs with. He won't want that information getting out."

"Thanks," I said. "I guess I owe you one."

"You can repay me by fixing whatever it is that's happening between you and April. I want this to be a happy family, okay?"

I nodded. "I'm trying, but it may be too late."

"You'll find a way. You're my son."

Mom kissed me on the cheek and then walked off into the kitchen to start cooking, as if nothing had happened. I tried to call April and tell her the good news, but she didn't answer. I didn't bother leaving a message. She ignored the ten previous ones I'd left.

"Foster, can I have a word?"

I spun round and saw Pierce standing at the top of the stairs. "I'm kind of busy right now," I lied.

"It won't take a minute."

I sighed, and walked up to the top of the stairs. No doubt Pierce had plenty to say to me after I'd effectively ruined his daughter's life.

"What is it?" I asked tersely.

"I overheard that conversation with your mom." *Shit.* "Why did you take the blame for all this? You covered for April's mistake."

Once again I tried to shrug casually, but even after practicing in the mirror it still came across as awkward and ungainly. Was it just physically impossible for someone of my size to shrug and look nonchalant?

"I'm the senior associate, and she's just a law student," I replied. "I have to take the blame when things go wrong."

"That's not it," Pierce said. "Kathleen said 'you don't have to be a genius to figure out why.' Unfortunately I'm not a genius. We both know that. So why don't you explain it to me."

Pierce was a lot cleverer than he was letting on. He might not have achieved much in his career, but he'd married two incredibly successful lawyers, so he couldn't be stupid. And right now he was playing me. Just like Mom, he'd figured out what was going on between April and me. He just wanted confirmation.

"She's family," I replied. "I felt duty-bound to cover for her."

"You're lying. There's covering for someone, and then there's going to a lot of effort to keep someone out of trouble and taking the blame yourself. You stood to get disbarred for this. I'll ask you again. Why did you do it?"

Pierce still sounded friendly, even as he accused me of lying to his face. He might not sound so friendly when he knows the truth.

"I did it because I... I did it because I love her. I'm in love with your daughter."

"You love April?" Pierce asked.

Now he did look shocked. Maybe he hadn't known after all. Or perhaps just didn't realize I loved her. I hadn't realized it myself until I said the words out loud.

"Yes. Yes, I do."

"I had no idea. I mean, I suspected there was something going on between you two, but I didn't realize you loved each other."

"We don't," I said reluctantly. "I love her, but the feeling isn't mutual."

Pierce smiled, and placed his hand on my shoulder. "You know, for someone who isn't short on experience with women, you don't really know a lot about them, do you?"

I knew a lot of intimate details about April, but Pierce probably didn't want to hear that. "What do you mean?"

"Just talk to her."

"She won't take my calls."

"Give her time. She's stubborn. She gets that from her mother."

"Thanks." Pierce smiled and headed downstairs. "Does this mean you don't mind?" I called out after him. "About April and I?"

"That remains to be seen. If you make her happy, then I'm fine with it. If you hurt her... well, let's just say that all the muscle and tattoos in the world can't counter the rage of an angry father."

I believed him.

I emailed April and told her that the situation was sorted. I didn't expect her to talk to me any time soon, but at least she wouldn't have to worry about her career.

I'd give her some space for a few days. There was something I needed to do. It might not be enough to make it up to her, but it was a start.

Chapter Thirty-Four

APRIL

I still had a career as a lawyer, but I wasn't sure I wanted one.

The law school told me to spend a week thinking over my decision. A career counselor called me to talk things through, but it didn't help much. I couldn't tell them all the details, so my career counselor just insisted that I would get another job easily with such stellar grades.

I read over Foster's email for the hundredth time. He'd been light on the details, but apparently Kathleen had fixed the situation. He'd left voicemails apologizing for being selfish and promising to make it up to me, but I'd not returned any of his calls.

Even Dad had been in touch to tell me not to go too hard on Foster. Was there anyone Foster couldn't charm?

Bryan found out I'd lost my job, although I'd no idea how, so he showed up at my apartment with a bottle of wine and a large tub of ice cream.

"Are you going to tell me what happened?" Bryan asked.

"Do I have to?"

"No, you don't *have* to. However, if you don't talk then I shall sit here and eat this ice cream without sharing any of it."

"That's not fair," I yelled, as I tried to grab a spoon from his hand. He held it out of reach and I didn't have the energy to fight him.

"Life's not fair," Bryan replied. "I thought you would have noticed that by now." He dug his spoon into the banana-flavored ice cream, and fed it slowly into his mouth. "This is *really* good, by the way."

"Fine, I'll tell you. There was a fuck up at work, and I ended up getting placed on a project that I'd already worked on for Cooper & Cooper representing the other side."

"Oh shit," Bryan remarked.

His face went serious and he quickly passed me a spoon. I dug into the ice cream and scooped out my reward.

"Yeah, 'oh shit' indeed. I don't know how I didn't realize, but I have such a bad memory for names, and I'd never been exposed to enough of the facts to spot that I was working on the same case."

"At least you didn't do anything corrupt. The only problem is how the situation looks to the ethics committee of whatever state bar you apply to. Unfortunately, they tend to come down hard on even the appearance of impropriety."

"The situation has been resolved. Kathleen sorted it all out. I don't know how, but she has."

"Oh, well, that's good. Isn't it?"

I nodded. "Sure."

"But you're still miserable, and cooped up in your apartment like an old cat lady, just without the cats."

"It's complicated."

"Problems with Foster."

I nodded again, but Bryan waited for me to give more details. Slowly but surely, he was teasing all the information out of me. "I thought we had something for a second. I even thought he felt the same way. I'm a complete idiot."

"You are most definitely not an idiot. You're the cleverest person I know, and I know some smart people."

"I should never have got involved with him. And to make things worse, he's my fucking stepbrother. I'm going to have to see him every Thanksgiving and Christmas, plus whatever other forced family events I get dragged along to."

"You should talk to him," Bryan said. "Just give him a chance to explain his side of events."

"I know what happened. He put his career before mine. I doubt he's lost any sleep over all this."

"I wouldn't be so sure about that if I were you."

Bryan had a guilty look on his face, like he'd said something he shouldn't. He ate another scoop of ice cream and tried to look calm, but I could tell he was hiding something.

"What's going on?" I asked.

"Nothing."

I snatched the spoon out of his hand, and held it out of his reach. "If you don't talk, I'm not going to let you eat any more ice cream."

"I can't say anything yet."

"Then you don't eat." I took the ice cream from Bryan and helped myself to another scoop, which I let slowly melt in my mouth, and added orgasmic noises for good effect.

"Alright, alright. All I'm saying is that you shouldn't be so quick to write him off. Foster's one of the good guys."

"He's a heartless corporate lawyer who doesn't give a shit about me or anyone else," I snapped back. The words sounded too cruel, but he'd made me feel that way. He only had himself to blame.

"That's not true. Just give him a chance."

"He's had enough chances," I replied.

"Hang in there," Bryan said. "I promise things are going to get better soon."

"They'd better," I said, as I handed Bryan back his spoon. He hadn't told me much, but if I ate all this ice cream by myself, I'd end up having to buy a new wardrobe with the last of my money from my summer working at Arrington & Hedges.

I checked my phone, but there were no messages or missed calls from Foster. He hadn't been in touch for days. Had he given up on me? I considered replying to one of his old messages, but it had been too long now.

When Bryan left, I tried to chill out in front of the television, but couldn't concentrate on anything. Every television show I watched reminded me of how shit my life was right now. I loved watching legal dramas, despite the inaccurate portrayal of life in a law firm, but they were a big no-go right now.

Similarly, any show with students in made me feel like shit, because they were always so optimistic. I wanted to scream at the screen, and tell them that life was hopeless and the real world sucked.

In the end, I picked up my laptop, and flicked through the prospectus for law school. I still intended to drop out, but if I was going to finish the third year, I needed to find some classes that actually interested me.

I thought I'd had this all planned out. I had a spreadsheet saved with all the classes I intended to take in my third year, but all those classes focused on a career in corporate law. There was no way I could spend a year studying for a career I didn't want.

While logged in to the law school's databases, I decided to check the court filings in the Jacob case to make sure Zach hadn't gone ahead and filed anything relating to Foster's fuck up with the conflict check.

Kathleen had apparently sorted it out, but if a motion had been filed with the court, then all her powers of persuasion wouldn't mean jack shit.

I didn't find anything. Just to be sure, I looked up Foster's legal profile on one of the legal search engines in case there was any mention of it there. Again, nothing showed up.

Just before I closed the tab, my eyes were drawn to the most recent filing under Foster's name. Yesterday he had filed a motion in the PorTupe case. There wasn't much unusual about that. In large cases like that one, motions were being filed on an almost weekly basis. Most of them were pointless, but this one was definitely not.

Foster had filed a motion to withdraw as legal counsel. That was a huge deal. While a client had free reign to pick and choose their attorney as they desired, attorneys had an obligation not to abandon their clients after commencing representation. Not to mention, the case would be in court soon, and that meant a chance in legal counsel would cause untold delays.

The court would tear Foster a new one for this.

I opened the motion and read through it quickly. The motion was short and to the point. Foster was withdrawing as legal counsel after uncovering information about the client that made it "unconscionable for me to continue as counsel."

No facts were included due to client confidentiality requirements, but I knew Foster was referring to the discrimination. He'd done it. He'd dropped his biggest client, and had done so at the worst possible time for them.

Bryan had been right. Foster deserved a second chance. The court might not give him one, but I sure as hell would.

Chapter Thirty-Five

FOSTER

Apparently doing the right thing could feel good. Shocking, huh?

April had found out about the motion I'd filed in the PorTupe case--probably because Bryan had a big mouth--and she'd got in touch to say she wanted to meet up.

I tried not to get too carried away, but knowing that I would be seeing her in just half an hour's time, gave me a warm glow inside that even my meeting with Zach couldn't disturb.

A few days ago, Zach had called to give me one last chance to pass PorTupe over to him in exchange for making this whole thing go away. Of course, I knew that he couldn't do anything with the information anyway, because his father had forbid it, but I didn't let him know that.

We met outside his office, and again he insisted on sneaking off somewhere quiet. The rumors about him having a broken jaw looked to be incorrect, but he still had one hell of a black eye. Well, not so much black any more, more a dingy yellow color. Either way, I actually took some pleasure in seeing his face for once. How many people could say that about Zach.

"I'm glad you finally came to your senses," Zach said.

He was trying to sound as cocky and smug as he had done the last time we'd met, but I could tell he was worried this wouldn't work out. He didn't have leverage anymore, so he had to hope I didn't call his bluff again.

"It's not too late for you to come to your senses," I said. "You can still call this off and we'll go our separate ways. You don't want to make an enemy of me."

My heart stopped in my chest as Zach paused and seemed to consider my offer. I'd only said that to make this seem more realistic, but he looked tempted.

"No," he said finally. A wave of relief washed over me, but I transformed it into a look of resignation for Zach's benefit. "We're doing this. And in case you haven't noticed, I'm not scared of you."

I twitched my right arm as if I were about to throw a punch, and Zach immediately backed up a few steps.

"Not afraid, huh?" I said, laughing.

"Whatever. I should make you pay for all the dental work I had to have done after the last time your temper got the best of you."

"It'd be worth the price."

"That's okay. I'm going to be rolling in money by the time all the new billings for PorTupe start coming in, and you might find you need to start cutting back."

"Can we just get this over with?" I asked, checking the time on my phone. "I have a meeting soon, and this conversation is boring me."

Zach smiled and looked giddy with excitement. He'd probably never brought in a new client before, let alone one as big as PorTupe. Right now he was likely picturing his new office, the promotions, and a fat paycheck.

If my plan had one notable drawback, it was that Zach might actually end up profiting from this. I didn't have to help him win PorTupe, but if he didn't get it then he might throw a temper tantrum and leak the information about April to the bar association. I didn't want that threat hanging over her. His dad had told him to stay quiet, but naughty children didn't always listen to their parents.

"Okay, how are we going to play this?" Zach asked. "I don't want this to take long."

"It won't. I've already resigned as legal counsel." I'd told PorTupe that I had personal issues to deal with. They'd never look at the motion I filed with the court, where I'd made it clear that my personal issue was very much related to the client.

"You have?" Again, I detected some hesitation from Zach, as if he could tell this was too easy.

"We'd just finished up a big project, so it seemed like the right time. I'll send them an email recommending he contact you for legal advice going forward."

"I want to see it," Zach said suspiciously.

I opened the email application on my phone and let Zach watch me type and send the email to PorTupe.

"I'm sure you'll be hearing from them shortly. Now, are you going to forget all about this incident with April?"

"You have my word."

"That's not worth a lot to me, but it will have to do. As you're so keen to remind me, I have a bit of a temper. You don't want to find out what I'll do if you ever go back on your promise."

Zach let his guard slip and for a few seconds I saw a glimpse of the fear in his eyes as he looked at me. Getting punched tended to have that effect. You relived the pain over and over again, until your fear of the pain became greater than the pain itself.

We were about to part ways, when I saw April walking straight towards us. Shit, this probably didn't look good. I hadn't told her my plan, and now she'd busted me talking to Zach.

April walked straight up to us, and she didn't exactly look pleased. "What's going on?"

"What's going on is that your boyfriend just handed me his biggest client," Zach said confidently. "You'll be pleased to know that you're in the clear. I'm going to drop this whole thing."

"You're too kind," April replied sarcastically. "It almost makes me wish I'd gone on that date with you after all."

"Don't flatter yourself. I never wanted to date you. I just like messing around with stuck-up little princesses. It helps pass the time at work, you know?"

I inhaled deeply, taking oxygen into my body to power my muscles, and then stepped forward to get in Zach's face. Did he get off on being punched? I considered myself well-versed in sexual kinks, but that was a new one to me.

April reached her hand between us and placed it on my chest, urging me to take a few steps back.

I moved back as she wanted, but remained within fist throwing range. Perhaps this time I actually would break his jaw.

"You're going to get what's coming to you one day," April said to Zach. "People like you always do."

"The only thing I have coming to me is a shitload of money. Just think, if you hadn't been such a frigid bitch, you could have been the lucky woman I shared my success with."

"You did not just call her that," I growled. My fists clenched by my side, but I didn't move my arms. April would kill me if I punched him. For some weird

242

reason, she didn't like physical violence, even against people like Zach.

"Call her what?" Zach asked. He looked me in eyes, challenging me to punch him. "Oh, I remember. Frigid bitch."

I envisioned my fist flying out and slamming into his pathetic face. He'd fall to the floor and scream, as blood and bits of teeth poured from his mouth.

But that didn't happen. I stayed still. Zach was just trying to rile me. He wanted a reaction. He wanted me to swing out and hit him in from of April.

I closed my eyes and took a deep breath and then another. Every muscle in my body was on fire, screaming out for me to do what came naturally when April was threatened. Finally, the fire receded and I relaxed.

"I'm impressed," April said. "You just exerted a phenomenal amount of self-control."

"Yeah, and it was exhausting," I replied. "Come on, let's get out of here before I have second thoughts."

"Sure," April said. "Just one moment."

She turned back to face Zach and swung out her arm punching him hard on the left side of his jaw. The same place I had hit him. Her technique had been a little sloppy, but like I said, all punches to the face hurt, and Zach had a low pain threshold.

"Looks like you'll be going back to the dentist," I remarked as he sank down to the floor holding his mouth.

I quickly ushered April away before we attracted too much attention from onlookers. "How's your fist?"

"I hurts like hell," she replied, examining her grazed knuckles. "I don't know how you do it."

"Sometimes the pain is worth it. You want a coffee."

"I want ice. And a strong drink."

I laughed. "In that case, let's go back to my place. We have a lot of catching up to do."

243

Chapter Thirty-Six

APRIL

I curled up on the sofa with Foster, relieved that we didn't have to keep our relationship a secret from our parents.

We still kept things tame in front of them though. If we ever got too affectionate, Dad and Kathleen would do the same, which tended to take both of us out of the mood pretty quickly. Dad found it hilarious.

The big day had finally arrived. Dad, Kathleen, Foster, and I, all huddled around the television to watch a press conference by the Department of Justice. Not exactly how most families spend their free time together.

While I had been sulking in my apartment and considering whether or not to drop out of law school, Foster had been busy putting together a bullet proof case for against PorTupe. He must have spent days pouring through all the emails on the system, but he'd found enough to warrant the DOJ opening an investigation.

The Attorney General stood up and gave his speech announcing that the DOJ had received substantial evidence from a whistleblower giving them reason to believe that PorTupe had engaged in a prolonged period of systemic discrimination against women and minorities.

Sat just to the side of the Attorney General, was a terrified looking Bryan who didn't look at home in front of the cameras. Foster had passed Bryan all the information, so internally Bryan had played a huge role in opening the investigation. He'd no doubt find himself pushed up a few pay grades by the time this was all over.

"How are things at work, Mom?" Foster asked. "I assume the partners are kicking up a right stink about this? Will you be able to keep your job?"

"Actually, it's not been that bad. Word got out that we resigned as counsel for ethical reasons, so although we've lost some clients, we've also gained quite a few. Some people like having an ethical lawyer, believe it or not. And most of the money from the PorTupe work went to you in the first place, so none of the partners have been hit too hard financially."

"It's a shame you didn't hang on to them, though," Dad said. "They're going to need a lot of legal advice over the next few years."

"That's what really bugs me," I said. "When all's said and done, Zach is going to profit from this just like he wanted."

"He sounds like a nasty piece of work," Dad remarked. "I wouldn't worry about it too much. People like him are never truly happy, no matter how much money they have."

"It still bugs me."

"Your dad's right," Foster said. "You shouldn't worry about it. Zach will get what's coming to him. I've planted a few seeds that should grow to fruition in the next few years."

"I don't like that sound of that," Kathleen remarked. "Do I want to hear this?"

"I do," Dad said eagerly. "Sounds juicy."

Kathleen rolled her eyes, but she didn't leave the room.

"All I've done is give Zach enough rope to hang himself," Foster said. "I had a word with the PorTupe directors and encouraged them to seek an alternate means of resolution to the case."

"You mean a bribe?" Dad asked.

"Maybe. I told him to go directly through Zach to get it sorted. Zach doesn't have to go along with it, but knowing him I think he will."

A few of the pieces clicked into place. "By any chance, did you mention that a good person to try and bribe was a young attorney going by the name of Bryan?"

Foster smiled. "My lips are sealed."

After the press conference, the media started speculating on what this investigation would mean for PorTupe. A few lawyers were dragged in to explain the process and how this would all play out. The short version is that this would take years to see through to its conclusion.

While the legal world moved at a glacial pace, the financial one didn't. PorTupe's stock price nose dived immediately after the press conference, wiping a third off its value in the space of a few hours.

The directors came under immediate pressure, but for the time being they refused to resign. That didn't bother me so much. The next few years would be a living hell for them, so it's not like they were getting off lightly.

"Time for us to make a move," Kathleen said, grabbing my dad's hand and encouraging him to stand up.

"Where are you going?" Foster asked.

"We're going to meet with a few of the partners in the New York office, to talk about me moving back here. Pierce is a large part of why I want to do that, so I'm taking him along."

Despite my dad's lack of experience in the corporate world, he never failed to impress other professionals after just a few minutes of casual conversation. He'd help Kathleen seal the deal.

"Have fun, you two," Dad said, as they left us alone on the sofa.

Foster gave me a little squeeze as I snuggled up on his chest. His muscles were firm, but the soft beating of his heart in his chest was almost hypnotic, and I often fell asleep on him while we were supposed to be watching television.

"Have I properly thanked you for everything you've done?" I asked.

"I consider what you did last night to be all the thanks I need. And the night before that. And the night before that."

"Well I mean it. You got me out of a big problem and sacrificed your own career in the process."

"I don't care. I'd do anything for you, April, you know that."

I did know that. I hadn't known Foster that long, but his actions spoke louder than words ever could.

We lay there in silence for a few more minutes while I tried to let everything soak in. The events of the past week were still a blur, and occasionally I thought I must have dreamed some or all of it. Remarkable things like that didn't happen to people like me.

I was a *magna cum laude* student; I wasn't supposed to be at the center of a big controversy. I was a plain looking girl; I wasn't supposed to end up in the arms of a man like Foster. Yet here I was.

I didn't even have to worry about Dad and Foster hating each other any more. The two of them were suddenly acting like the best of friends, and it appeared to be genuine.

"What did you say to my dad to get him to like you so much?" I asked Foster.

For once, Foster's heart rate actually sped up. Had I touched on a sensitive subject? I sat up and looked at him. If I didn't know better, I could have sworn he looked nervous and apprehensive.

I'd never seen Foster go red before, but there were hints of color on his tanned cheeks. It was completely adorable, not to mention reassuring to know that he was human after all.

"I had a word with your father," Foster said eventually.

"Did you apologize properly this time?"

"No, not exactly." He turned to look at me. His eyes were serious, and for a fleeting moment I felt certain he was going to give me bad news. Then he smiled. "I told your dad I loved you."

"Oh." *He loves me?* I didn't think Foster did love, but then love really did work in mysterious ways.

"'Oh?' Is that all you want to say?"

I couldn't feel his heart rate anymore, but if I could, it would be racing a mile a minute and about to burst through his chest.

"I don't know what to say," I said.

"Ah. Well, never mind then."

Foster turned away and tried to act like he didn't care. He was cute when he was upset.

"I don't know what to say, because so far you've only told my father and not me."

"But I just told... You're going to make me say it aren't you?"

"Say what?" I asked with mock look of uncertainty on my face.

"April Rhodes," Foster said, taking my hand. "I love you."

"That's better," I said, kissing him on the cheek. I looked away and pretended to read something on my phone.

"April?"

I threw my phone down on the sofa and turned back to face him. "Yeah, I love you too. Now come here and kiss me."

"I'm going to do a lot more than that."

Chapter Thirty-Seven

APRIL

Foster carried me up to the bedroom. Apparently I moved far too slow for his liking.

He threw me down on the bed and immediately tugged my jeans off my legs. I lifted my top over my head and then enjoyed the view as I watched Foster peel off his tight t-shirt to reveal the toned muscle underneath.

His pants dropped to the floor soon after as he crawled between my legs and started kissing my thighs the same way he had done last summer. I hadn't even known his name back then. So much had changed since that night, but not the way warmth spread through my body in anticipation whenever Foster got close to my sex.

Just like last summer, I couldn't handle the teasing. Every time his tongue got close to my panties, I tried to thrust my sex in his face, hoping he would tear off my underwear with his teeth and start exploring my wetness.

I locked my legs behind his back to trap him, but my thighs were no match for his strength. His lips kissed my skin, leaving behind a feeling of satisfaction wherever they landed, and reminding me how much I wanted them elsewhere.

I growled in frustration as Foster kissed my mound through my panties.

"You're still not very patient, are you?" Foster said, looking up at me from between my legs with a grin covering his face.

"And you're still a tease," I replied. "Now stop playing around and eat me."

He maintained eye contact with me as his fingers hooked under my panties and pulled them down my legs. He held my panties up to his face and sniffed them, still looking at me as he did so.

One thing had changed since last summer; I now made sure to wear nicer panties.

"You smell so good," he remarked. "I might have to keep this pair for my collection as well."

"I taste even better." My foot reached up and I took hold of the panties between my toes, yanking them out of Foster's hands and letting them fall to the floor. "Lick me. Now."

Foster finally put me out of my misery. His tongue went straight between my folds and stretched into my entrance as he tasted my eagerness.

I threw the pillows off the bed and laid flat on my back as Foster went to work between my legs. His tongue moved slowly up and down my slit while a finger opened my sex and teased me with what was to come when something much longer and thicker entered me.

Each time his tongue reached the top of my lips, Foster pressed it firmly against my throbbing clit, knowing I would thrust my sex against him in a desperate need for more. He knew how to press all my buttons, and he know how to drag it out as well. Foster always made me come, but not until he wanted me to.

His hands took a firm hold of my thighs, pressing down against the bed to stop me from squirming. He took my clit between his lips and sucked gently, lashing his tongue against it in a series of light flicks that always sent me over the edge.

Sparks spread throughout my body, making every muscle in my body tense, from my toes to my fingers. I was helpless under Foster's tongue.

Then he stopped.

I gasped, panting for breath and on the edge of coming. I looked down between my legs, and saw Foster coming towards me, his face glistening with my essence.

"You haven't finished yet," I pleaded. "Just a little longer."

"You'll come when I tell you to come."

His lips crashed into mine. I thrust my tongue in his mouth to greedily taste the wetness that I had left over his face. It drove me wild to know what I'd done to him and it nearly tipped me over the edge, even without any physical contact between my legs.

I reached my hand down, intending to finish the job myself. Foster had watched me do it before and it ended much the same way as any other orgasm; with him fucking me senseless.

"No," he yelled, grabbing my wrist. "Stop misbehaving you naughty girl."

I bit my lip and watched as he walked over to the drawers and grabbed a condom.

"You don't need that," I said. "We don't have to use those. I'm on the pill and I trust you."

"Thank fuck for that," he replied, throwing the condom to the floor. "Because I've been dying to fill up that pussy for quite some time."

Foster held my legs open and pressed my thighs up towards his chest. I looked into his eyes, as the tip of his cock rubbed against my folds until it found the opening. He paused and then plunged into my wetness.

"Fuck," I yelled out, snapping my head back as his cock completely filled me up. Without the thin rubber of the condom, I could feel the throbbing of his penis inside me, like a ticking time-bomb ready to explode.

"This feels so good, baby," Foster groans. "I can feel your wetness soaking my cock."

His heavy balls slapped against my ass with each thrust, as his head rubbed against my upper wall bringing me back to the brink.

I reached out and grabbed hold of his arms, digging my nails into his flesh, so he could feel how close I was. I tried to pull him closer to me, but he resisted. The more I tried to finish the more he fought me.

My sex contracted and squeezed around his member, as if trying to milk the cum from his tip. I saw Foster's resistance slipping and knew he was close as well.

Foster leaned forward and whispered in my ear. "You can come now."

I gave in to him. He thrust himself deep inside me. My vision went blurry and suddenly the only sound I could hear was our heavy breathing. It was like we were the only two people in the word.

I came without making a sound, other than my fingers clenching the sheets and my body convulsing on the bed.

My vision was still blurry, but I felt Foster thrust deep into my core as he emptied himself inside me. His cock stayed hard, as he lay on top of me, looking into my eyes as we both recovered from our orgasms.

Eventually he pulled his cock from me, leaving me feeling less whole, like something was now missing. His essence dribbled out of my pussy and trickled down the insides of my thighs.

Foster collapsed onto his back, but I wasn't quite finished. I crawled on top of him and worked my way down to his member which was still firm but gradually going flaccid. It was covered in my juices and his own cum.

"What are you--" Foster started asking, before I interrupted him by taking his cock in my mouth. I devoured the mixture of our juices, and sucked him hard, making the most of a rare opportunity to fit the whole of him in my mouth. Just.

"I wasn't expecting that," Foster said, after I'd licked his cock clean.

"You like?"

"Oh, I like."

"Good. I'll do it again next time. On one condition."

"Which is?" Foster asked quizzically.

"You let me come in your face."

Foster smiled. "Alright. I guess I can live with that."

Chapter Thirty-Eight

APRIL

I wanted to kill whoever designed graduation gowns.

Or whoever thought it was a good idea to cram thousands of people inside a hall and have them sit there for hours with no air conditioning on a day when the temperature approached one hundred degrees.

Either way, I wanted to kill *someone*. I couldn't help it; I got grumpy when I was hot and sweaty in public.

At least I didn't have to give a speech. I'd just missed out on one of the top three spots in my graduating year, which made me furious until I remembered that I didn't care anymore.

I was so used to grades being the be all and end all--the thing that defined me as a person--that the new me hadn't quite gotten used to not caring.

I'd gone back through all my exams and considered challenging the grades my professors had given me to see if I could get another 0.02 onto my GPA and scrape into the top three.

Then it hit me--it didn't matter. I already had a job lined up for after graduation, and my new employer didn't care about my grades. All I had to do was pass the bar exam, which compared to everything I'd been through in the last couple of years should be a walk in the park.

Another old habit I'd struggled to break was always worrying about money. I didn't have to do that anymore, but a lifetime of careful budgeting was hard to escape.

When I'd been considering dropping out of law school, Dad sat down with me and asked me whether I really wanted to become a lawyer. I'd answered yes immediately because it was true. My decision to go into corporate law had been influenced by my mom, but becoming a lawyer was still a passion of mine. I didn't want to give it up.

Dad had then asked what areas of law really excited me. There weren't many, but one class caught my eye. Constitutional Law II. The class was taught by a professor who had argued in front of the Supreme Court, and it covered freedom of speech and equal rights.

I told Dad I wanted to stick up for the little guy. I sounded like a naive schoolgirl. At least half of my colleagues had started law school with the dream of becoming a constitutional lawyer, but then little things like soul-crushing debt had popped up to pay a visit and suddenly they were all chasing the big law firm jobs.

With my grades, I would be able to get a job, but it wouldn't pay well. The little guy couldn't pay legal bills.

"You don't need to worry about money any more, sweetie," Dad had said.

At first, I'd thought he meant I could just live off Kathleen, which I had absolutely no intention of doing, but then he explained about Mom's insurance policy.

I was rich. Sort of. The money wouldn't last forever, but it would keep me going for a really long time. I planned to pay off my student debt straight away, and then invest the rest of it. Perhaps I could put some aside for a few nice vacations with Foster.

Foster hadn't worked in nine months, but he hadn't exactly sat around the house either. He'd put that massive brain to use, and signed up to help out at legal aid clinics. He sat at a table and helped out whoever walked through the door with whatever random legal issue they had.

And he loved it.

He wouldn't do it forever, mind you. There had already been a few signs of impatience creeping in. He'd helped me out with schoolwork a lot, and gave Kathleen regular consultations just so he could keep in the game. He'd be back at a firm one day, but for now he was making up for years of chasing money over everything else, and it made him happy.

I looked for Foster in the crowd as I joined the line to collect my diploma. Foster usually stood out in a crowd, but the hall was packed and I couldn't see him anywhere.

As the dean called my name a loud cheer went up from near the front of the crowd to my right hand side. I looked over and saw Foster standing there banging his hands together loud enough that most people in the hall were turning to look at him.

I collected my diploma and got shuffled back into the audience after taking the mandatory cheesy photo with the law school's photographer.

The ceremony took another thirty minutes, but at least now I had Foster to look at while I daydreamed about what we would do when I finally got these God-damned robes off. Well, first I would have a shower, but after that we could have some fun and make the most of the last week in my apartment before we moved into our new place near Capitol Hill.

It had cost a small fortune and taken a chunk out of Mom's money, but it would be worth it to have somewhere to live with Foster.

I couldn't wait to get out of the robes, but after the ceremony, everyone wanted to have their picture taken with the graduates. I hung out with law school friends for a bit. They all wanted to meet Foster, but Kathleen and Dad had to hide the fact they were a couple. Law students were a judgmental bunch and I didn't need that information flying around before I'd even got off the campus.

"Want to go for a walk?" Foster asked. "I'm starting to remember why I didn't enjoy law school. Do these people ever stop? I heard one of them talking about how he's going to go home and start studying for the bar exam *this evening.*"

I laughed. "Actually, I was thinking--"

"Oh hell no. I want two whole days with you before you become a stressed-out nightmare to be around."

"One day," I bargained.

"One day, but two nights."

"Deal. Where do you want to go?"

"Let's just walk down to the National Mall and hang out by the Washington Monument."

"Trust you to pick the phallus shaped object," I pointed out.

"Hey, it's the only 'phallus shaped object' in this city bigger than the one in my pants. I feel inadequate around it, which must be how normal men feel around me."

"Sometimes I wonder how I ever fell in love with someone so arrogant."

"Yeah, but then I get you in bed and you remember."

I couldn't argue with that. We strolled down to the Washington Monument, and somehow Foster managed to get tickets to go up to the top even though it was always sold out well in advance.

The view from the top was like nothing I've ever seen before. You got a good view of D.C. coming in on a plane to Reagan Airport, but that didn't compare to standing in the middle of the Mall and looking around at the nation's capital where all the magic happened. Or *sometimes* happened when people could agree on things. For a budding young lawyer, it was an absolute inspiration.

Foster stood behind me and wrapped his arms around me. Even up here his mind was only on one thing, so I had to slap his hand away as it crept down between my legs.

"Give it ten years and you'll be a famous name in this town," he whispered in my ear.

"I don't want to be famous. I want to make a difference."

"You'll do both. I'm sure of it."

"What about you?" I asked. "Are you going back to work soon?"

I hadn't told Foster this, but I didn't want him rushing back to being a full-time lawyer again. I didn't want him working late, and being stressed out all the time. That was my job, especially while I studied for the bar exam.

"Not yet," he replied. "I figure you'll need some support while you study, so I want to be around to cook you meals and remind you to get some fresh air occasionally. Besides, planning for the wedding will keep me busy."

"Mmm," I murmured, sinking back into his chest as he held me tightly in his arms. Then I snapped out of it. "Wait, what wedding?"

"Hopefully ours," Foster said. "Assuming you say yes."

A small box appeared in front of me, which Foster flicked open to reveal a large diamond. The sun shone through the opening in front of us and illuminated it perfectly, letting me appreciate the rock in all its natural beauty.

Is this real? I'd accepted that being with Foster meant I wouldn't get a romantic proposal, or a big white wedding. Foster wasn't the type for grand gestures and romance. Or so I'd thought.

"I know it's soon," Foster said, breaking the uneasy silence. "But I do not have a single doubt in my mind about this. I've never wanted anything this much."

"I can't believe we're going to do this."

"Is that a yes?"

"Dad's going to go nuts."

"April? Answer the damn question."

"Of course it's a yes."

I threw my arms around him and pulled him towards me for a kiss. We held each other tightly, our lips not parting, until the guide politely coughed and informed us that we need to make our way back down.

I was still staring at the ring on my finger when we made it back outside where Kathleen and Dad were waiting for us.

"I'm going to assume from the smile on your face and that massive rock on your finger, that you said yes?" Dad asked.

"Did you know?"

"Foster is apparently more traditional than I gave him credit for. He asked for my permission."

"Good Lord, my son is growing up," Kathleen joked.

"Don't get carried away," Foster said. "If Pierce had said no, I'd still have asked her anyway."

We held hands as we walked off to find somewhere to eat. I didn't make important decisions just to make Mom proud anymore, but I had a feeling she would be pretty damn pleased with how things had turned out.

Dad was happy, and I was ecstatic. I couldn't say my life was perfect--not without Mom--but life was damn good right now.

I had a feeling it would only get better.

Epilogue

Three Years Later

APRIL

"You scared?" Foster asked.

I nodded. The nerves never went away.

"Come on, you know what to do," Foster teased.

I smiled and placed my hand on his chest. I did this before every court appearance to calm my nerves. Something about feeling his heartbeat always helped me relax ever since that first courtroom appearance in the Doris case.

My one regret about not working for Arrington, Arrington, & Hedges was that I'd had to drop the hunt for Doris' son. At least Foster was still working on it, and by some miracle Doris was still clinging on to life. There was hope for a happy ending yet.

"Okay, I'm good," I said, picking up my materials and walking into the court. Foster took his usual seat in the audience.

This was my fifteenth appearance representing a client in a courtroom, and my third in front of Judge

Whiteman. I still had the same butterflies in my stomach that had kept me awake the night before the first trial.

"Good to see you again, Mrs. Arrington," Judge Whiteman said as I introduced myself to the court. "I enjoyed reading your brief, although not as much as that one you filed a few years ago."

Every time. Every fucking time I saw Judge Whiteman he slipped in a little reminder of that brief. If I ever did become famous, he was going to make a fortune telling that story on the after-dinner circuit around D.C.

"I'll try to spice it up a bit next time," I replied.

Today was my first jury trial. I had to convince six people that my client had suffered severe discrimination in the workplace, such that she'd had to resign and had suffered a mental breakdown.

I'd practically had a panic attack when the case had first landed on my desk. We were going up against a large department store that had retained a law firm almost as big as Arrington, Arrington, & Hedges.

Fortunately, the big law firm had taken one look at me and figured this would be a walk in the park. They didn't prepare properly and I locked the case down in jury selection. The actual trial would be a formality now.

Opposing counsel had been so obsessed with keeping women and minorities off the jury, who would supposedly be biased against the defendant, that they hadn't bothered asking the jurors many questions.

That allowed me to slip through a juror whose wife had won a case for discrimination, a man who'd been fired from the department store a few months ago, and three other people who described themselves as staunchly in favor of increased protection for employees in the workplace.

I had this case in the bag.

In addition to having the jurors on my side, I also had my lucky charm in the audience. Foster had been to every single one of my court appearances, even though he was now a partner at Arrington, Arrington, & Hedges.

He'd been welcomed back into the fold once it became clear that PorTupe was a complete shambles. As Foster had predicted, Zach tried to bribe Bryan and other lawyers at the DOJ, which went down about as well as you can imagine.

The ensuing scandal nearly took Cooper & Cooper into bankruptcy, but at the last minute they merged with another firm in the corporate field. The competent attorneys from Cooper & Cooper stayed on at the new firm, but Zach got booted out within the month.

I had a feeling he'd worm his way out of the bribery prosecution, but he wouldn't work as a lawyer again either way. I had zero sympathy for him. He'd made his bed, now he had to lie in it.

The trial went smoothly, even though I nearly lost my way during the closing argument. We won the case convincingly which hopefully meant opposing counsel wouldn't bother trying to find grounds for an appeal. By the time the case made it to an appellate court, I would be on leave from work and wouldn't be able to handle the case.

"Great work, baby," Foster said, once we were outside the courtroom. He kissed me on the cheek and put his hand on the small of my back.

"Thanks." I had to tell him the news today. I'd thrown up the last three mornings, but he'd already left for work each time. He'd catch me soon enough though.

"How about we go grab a drink?" Foster asked.

It would have to be non-alcoholic. "Sure. Where do you want to go?"

"How about we go back to the rooftop bar near my office?"

"Back to where it all began?" I asked.

"I have very fond memories from that night."

"Me too. And I think after tonight you'll have some more."

"What does that mean?" he asked.

"You'll find out soon enough." I touched my stomach unconsciously, even though there was no bump to give away the secret just yet.

Foster and I argued a fair bit, but we always made up quickly and passionately. It came with the territory of being two busy lawyers. One argument we wouldn't need to have was the baby name. If it was a boy, we would name him Steve after Foster's dad. If it was a girl, we would name her Laura, after Mom.

Boy or girl, the baby was going to be spoiled rotten by Foster, and our parents. That kid would never want for a thing.

Neither would I. Not with Foster.

"I love you," Foster said, out of the blue, as we walked to the bar.

"I love you too," I replied. He was going to be a great dad.

THE END

Also by Jessica Ashe

Check out Jessica Ashe's debut novel, Escape, available now.

Here's a sneak preview of the book:

A Note on Language

Escape tells the story of Victoria and Caiden. Victoria is English and therefore her chapters are written with British English spelling and idioms. Conversely, Caiden is American and therefore his chapters are written with American English spelling and idioms.

Chapter One
VICTORIA

The man flashed a grin at me as he walked out of the convenience store clutching a large box of condoms. Caiden? It couldn't be him. I'd been seeing his face everywhere since I lost my virginity to him last week. I must have been imagining things.

Caiden couldn't be here. Not in my local corner shop a hundred miles from where he was staying in London.

There was no mistaking that grin, though. It screamed 'I'm a cocky, arrogant, arsehole who's in love with my own reflection.'

That grin had charmed most of the girls I went to school with, and a few of them even ended up going back to his penthouse in London for drunken one-night stands.

So had I. He'd grinned at me like that when I'd undressed in front of him last week just before he took my virginity.

Snap out of it Victoria, you're imagining things. Caiden was living in London for the summer and would soon be returning home to America. Why would he be in my sleepy little town?

"You okay, Victoria?" Betty asked, as she took the bread, cheese, and cold meat from my shopping basket.

Betty had been working in this shop for as long as I could remember. When we first came here as a small child, Betty had owned the small, independent store, and she worked seven days a week all year round.

At some point, a big supermarket chain had noticed the prestigious piece of real estate in Windsor and had purchased the shop from Betty. I'd felt sorry for her at first. She'd cried when they took the sign down and changed the name, but a few weeks later she looked noticeably happier. She only had to work five days a week now and she once told me she preferred being bossed around than being the boss herself.

"Yeah, yeah, I'm fine. Thanks, Betty," I replied.

"You look like you've seen a ghost," Betty said. "That'll be £7.65."

"I'm just tired from the journey home," I said, as I slid my debit card in the chip and pin machine. Caiden was no ghost. A ghost wouldn't have given me the best night of my life. I shuddered as I thought back to the moment he entered me; temporary pain quickly giving way to wave after wave of pleasure.

I hadn't done much that first time other than just lay there. He had done all the work, but he was the expert after all. I made up for it the second time. And the time after that.

"I'm sure your father will be delighted to have you back home," Betty said. "I always ask after you whenever he comes in here, and he tells me how well you're doing at school. I hear you're off to uni in a few months? Cambridge is it?"

I nodded. I hadn't told my dad I'd been accepted by the University of Cambridge, but he'd already gone around telling everyone about it as if it were a done deal. Typical.

"Yes," I replied, taking the food and slipping it into my backpack. I looked behind me to check that no-one was waiting to pay. "This might sound like an odd question, but did the last customer have an American accent?"

"I don't know," Betty replied. "He just put the condoms down and paid without saying a word. Come to think of it, his card wouldn't work in the pin machine and I'd never heard of the bank on the card. I guess he could have been American. I know one thing about him though."

"What's that?" I asked.

Betty motioned for me to lean in closer. "He's got one hell of a nice arse and he's just bought a big box of condoms. Why don't you go out there and introduce yourself?"

"Betty!" I exclaimed, immediately blushing red like I was still the virgin I had been a week ago. "I'm not going to sleep with some strange guy." Not again. Never again. "Especially not one covered in tattoos."

Betty shrugged. "You're going to university soon. You're bound to do it sooner rather than later. I'll tell you this, none of the boys at Cambridge—and that's what they will be, boys— will get your blood rushing half as much as a man like that."

How right she was. Caiden had done things to me that I didn't think were possible and for the last week I had been trying and failing to replicate that experience myself. I hadn't even come close.

"I won't tell your father," Betty added. "Just promise me you'll try to live a little this summer, okay? It's the last few months of freedom you'll have in a while."

"I promise. But I might stick to hanging out with friends and cooking, instead of... doing that other stuff."

Betty smiled and shook her head. "If you make any of those pear muffins again, you be sure to stop by. Don't be a stranger."

I left the store and looked around for Caiden. I must be going mad. It was basically impossible for him to be here. He never left London and on the rare occasions I had spoken to him, he had made his disdain for the English countryside quite clear. Windsor wasn't the countryside, but it was a relatively small town and to Caiden they were all the same. For him, it was London or nothing.

I couldn't see Caiden. I sat down on a bench and tried to reassure myself that he wasn't here and that I would never need to see him again.

In three months, I would be going to the University of Cambridge and would leave my old life far behind. No more all-girls school, no more uniform, and no more bumping into Caiden every time my friends insisted on going to a club. I would happily never go to London again if that's what it took to avoid Caiden.

I opened up my backpack and took out the letter that I had kept immaculately pressed between two cookbooks that I'd brought home with me from boarding school.

The envelope had the University of Cambridge logo in the corner, so there had been no mistaking what was inside. The official acceptance would come from UCAS soon after, but Cambridge insisted on writing to all applicants separately if they were accepted.

I looked at the letter again. The dean praised my application using generic language which he clearly sent to all applicants and then confirmed that I had been accepted for a place to read—not study, *read*—Philosophy, Politics, and Economics. PPE. The same course my dad had taken decades ago.

At the bottom of the letter, the dean had scribbled a few words next to his signature. "I loved your personal statement. You'll be a great addition to our university." That was a nice touch, but I couldn't shake the suspicion that he wrote that on every letter.

My personal statement had been one of the strongest parts of my application. My expected A-level grades were two A stars and three As. Good grades without a doubt, but fairly standard among Cambridge applicants.

My personal statement definitely had an emotional element to it. I wrote about my experience after my mum was nearly killed in a car crash. She'd spent months in intensive care and, even though she was now out of hospital, she had never been the same since. She'd get better one day, but that could be years away.

My dad had somehow arranged for a divorce the second she was deemed capable of giving consent, and I'd chosen to live with him. Not because I got on with my father better than my mother—I couldn't stand him most of the time—

but because my mother could barely look after herself. I didn't want to inflict more pressure on her while she recovered.

I stood up and began the short walk home. My bag was heavy with the books and food, so I decided to run across the busy street by the corner shop instead of walking up to the crossing. A gap in the cars appeared, so I quickly darted across, my head constantly looking both ways.

I made it two-thirds of the way over when I saw Caiden again. Only from behind this time, but it was unmistakably him. I'd recognize the triangular shape of his back anywhere and the tattoo on the back of his neck was visible even from fifty feet away. He was walking in a different direction to me, but that was him.

A car horn blared and snapped me out of my trance. I was still standing in the middle of the street and a car had come to a screeching halt in front of me. *Well done Victoria. You're mother's nearly killed in a car accident and yet you decide to stop in the middle of a busy street.*

I waved a hand apologetically and skipped to the pavement. I turned to look at Caiden again. He'd turned around and was now walking straight towards me. He was looking down at his phone and hadn't seen me.

I lowered my gaze and kept walking back towards my house. My hand gripped hold of the Cambridge acceptance letter and I tried to focus on the task at hand. My father had summoned me home for an urgent meeting, but I had news of my own to tell him. I didn't want to go to Cambridge. I didn't want to go to university at all. Not yet at least. Maybe not ever. That was going to be tough news for him to take.

I approached another road to cross. In just a few minutes I would be back home. Back in my childhood house for the first time since Christmas. The road was quiet, but I still flicked my head both ways before crossing. Nothing like nearly being run over to make you more cautious crossing the road.

My right foot moved to step out onto the road when I felt a finger tap me on the shoulder. I stopped and turned around. Caiden. I looked straight into the deep blue eyes of the man that had taken my virginity a week ago. The eyes that I'd gazed into as I orgasmed with a man for the first time.

"Hi Vicky," Caiden said. "You miss me?"

"What are you doing here?" I snapped at him through gritted teeth. No-one was around to hear us, but you never knew if there was a nosey neighbour looking out the window.

"You were much more pleased to see me last time," Caiden said, his grin still lighting up his smug face. "If I remember correctly, you walked in and started getting undressed immediately. By this point I could already see those pert little titties of yours. Are you going to get your tits out for me again? I wouldn't mind another look even though they are a bit underwhelming."

Underwhelming? He hadn't seemed underwhelmed with them last week. He hadn't been able to take his hands off them. I thought back to how he grasped them firmly while I'd been riding him. His thumb and forefinger squeezed my nipples until I moaned and dug my nails into his chest. He'd sucked greedily on them and even used his teeth on my nipples as they stiffened in

279

his mouth. I'd pressed my nails deeper into his chest as the pain shot through me, but I never told him to stop. I didn't want him to stop.

"You need to get the hell out of here," I yelled, not bothering to keep my voice down anymore. "Why are you following me anyway? How do you even know where I live? Are you stalking me?"

"You really think I'd stalk you? You have a high opinion of yourself, don't you? I don't make a habit of chasing after women—they chase after me. Even if I did, I certainly wouldn't bother with you, although given how little you moved that night, I reckon you'd be quite easy to catch."

"Why are you following me then?" I asked. I tried to ignore his insult, but it rang true. The first time we fucked I'd just lain there and let him have his way with me. I had been so overcome with what was happening, it hadn't occurred to me to do anything. I'd more than made up for it the second time though. And the third. Hadn't I? He'd seemed satisfied enough at the time, but I was probably kidding myself. How good in bed could I have been compared to all the more experienced women he usually slept with?

"I told you, I'm not following you."

"You just happen to be in my home town on the day I am coming home for the summer? That would be one heck of a coincidence."

"Stranger things have happened," Caiden said. "Like a silly little virgin coming up to me and asking for sex even though she'd seemed like a stuck up little madam before."

"I wasn't a virgin," I lied. I hadn't wanted him to know, but it had probably been obvious.

Perhaps I should admit to it. At least then I would have an excuse for not being good enough in bed.

Why did I care what he thought of my performance? The entire point of that night had been to loose my V plates to someone I didn't care about. It's not like I wanted to sleep with him again. Did I?

"You *were* a virgin, but that's fine. I consider it part of my civic duty to deflower as many English virgins as possible before I go back to the US."

"Why don't you just shove off back to the States then? I think I speak for all English women when I say we don't want you."

" 'Shove off?' " Adrian asked, mocking my choice of words. "Aren't you the polite one. I think the words you were looking for were 'fuck off.' You remember that word, right? *Fuck*?"

"I don't need to use vulgar language to get my point across," I replied, crossing my arms over my chest and pushing up my tiny breasts in the process. Not that he could see them anyway. I wore a cardigan that was buttoned up enough to completely cover my chest even though it was easily warm enough to go without.

"Oh really? In that case, when I took your virginity you should have been saying 'oh yes, put your penis inside my vaginal canal with more speed and pressure.' Was that what you said? I'm sure it was more along the lines of 'oh yes, fuck me. Fuck me. Harder, harder.' "

I cringed as I thought back to the third time we'd fucked that night. The second time I had been on top of him and ridden him hard, but I'd still not said a lot. The third time, something had come over me and I'd moaned in the same way porn stars did. Presumably.

What if someone in the room next door had heard us? I must have sounded like a complete slut.

"I'm going to walk home now," I said slowly. I was blushing furiously, but there wasn't much I could do about that so I ignored it. "Don't you dare follow me."

"Vicky," Caiden said as he grabbed my wrist.

I turned and yanked my hand free from his wrist before placing both hands on his chest and pushing him hard. He stumbled back with a shocked look in his face and ended up in the bush behind him.

I nearly apologised out of habit, but then forced a smile and turned for home. My childhood house was located off the main roads and down a long driveway. We lived on the outskirts of town, and with such a long driveway we were fairly secluded from most other houses. I often saw envious looks from nearby residents as they peered up the driveway to catch a glimpse of the house and the surrounding land.

As I walked up the driveway, I noticed a second car parked next to my dad's silver Mercedes. My knowledge of cars extended to recognizing the difference between some with three doors and some with five, but that was about it. This car looked brand new and more expensive than my dad's which meant he would soon go out and buy a new one soon. He hated having friends with a nicer car than his.

The new car had the familiar logo of a rental company on the back window. Rented cars were a familiar enough site around London, but not many tourists came visiting our little town.

I dug my keys out of my bag, but the front door opened before I needed to use them. My dad stood in the doorway and beamed with pride at seeing me return. Something must be wrong. Dad never looked at me like that. He would never say as much, but he didn't actually like having me at home. I got in his way. The last time I'd come back he'd completely forgotten about it and gone on a golfing holiday to Italy with some friends.

"Victoria, welcome home," he said with feigned enthusiasm.

It was then I noticed the woman standing behind him. A blonde lady, with a generous bosom, and an even more generous helping of make up. My first thought was that she looked like a TV personality. My second thought was that I recognized her. I was right on both counts, although I mainly knew her face from books not television.

The woman smiled at me and held out her hand. "Hello Victoria, I'm Sheri Ramsden."

"I know who you are, Ms Ramsden," I replied, shaking her hand excitedly. "I'm a big fan." Sheri was a famous chef and I had one of her cookbooks in my bag right now. I just barely resisted the temptation to ask for her autograph until I knew why she was here.

Sheri looked over my shoulder and her face turned sour. "There you are," she said sternly. "Where have you been?"

I looked over and saw Caiden standing there openly holding his box of condoms.

"Don't panic, I'm here now," Caiden said calmly, walking into my house as if he owned the place. "So what was it you wanted to talk about? This had better be important, Mum."

Chapter Two

VICTORIA

Dad ushered us all inside and told Caiden and I to go and sit in the lounge. I didn't intend to be alone in the same room as him, but when Sheri walked in as well I decided it would be safe to follow.

Dad went to make some cups of tea for everyone, which immediately put me on edge. Dad was acting far too nice; he never made tea, even when we had guests. When Mum was around he would tell her to do it and now that she no longer lived with us he would usually have me make the drinks.

Sheri sat down on the middle of the sofa, but didn't look entirely comfortable. She wouldn't look at either Caiden or me and she kept picking at her fingers as if nervous.

I sat down in the armchair that used to be Mum's favourite seat and Caiden sat on the ottoman. He immediately pulled out his phone and began typing away as if he didn't have a care in the world. Surely he must be wondering what was going on as well? Or did he already know?

I'd grown up in this house yet right now I felt like a stranger, especially with Sheri sat to my left. I'd admired her ever since I started taking cooking seriously and it wouldn't be an exaggeration to say that I wanted to be like her one day. On any other occasion I would be delighted to have her in my home, but Caiden had ruined that for me.

He didn't even have the decency to take his shoes off before coming inside. How could he be Sheri's son? Sheri always looked immaculately dressed and, while that was sometimes for the camera, she still carried an air of sophistication about her that was the polar opposite from the debauched way Caiden looked and dressed.

In addition to the tattoo on the back of his neck, I could also see the ones going down his entire right arm all the way to the wrist. I thought back to when I had first seen him naked and remembered that the arm tattoo was connected to the one on his neck. He also had a tattoo on his right calf although that was covered by his jeans at the moment.

Next to Caiden on the ottoman was Caiden's large box of condoms that he had just thrown down there as if it was just a pack of gum. We'd only had sex a week ago and I distinctly remembered there had been at least five condoms left in the packet when I bailed from the hotel in the morning. Obviously he hadn't been lying when he said I didn't keep him satisfied.

I felt a twinge of jealousy in my chest as I pictured him with other women. I didn't care about the ones before me. I'd picked him solely because he had experience with other women. Well, that and the biceps that my eyes couldn't look away from. And the muscular back. And the messy, dishevelled hair that just begged for me to run my hands through it. Just those things.

I ached as I pictured other girls pulling his hair as they fucked. In my head, I heard Caiden tell them how much better they were than me. He probably screwed them in all sorts of positions we never got to like 'doggy style' and... other ones. They'd probably given him head too.

Why hadn't I given him a blow job? I'd been so selfish. No wonder he had to get his satisfaction elsewhere after me. I remembered going down towards his penis and seeing it close up after we'd screwed. It was a good job I hadn't seen it in its full glory before he put it inside me; I'd have chickened out and run a mile.

I'd heard the rumours of him being well-hung, but I hadn't known what well-hung truly entailed. Say one thing about me, when I do things, I don't do them in half measures. I didn't lose my virginity to a fellow virgin with an average penis. I lost it with an experienced guy with a monster cock.

Finally Dad came back into the room carrying a tray with four cups of tea on it. I raised my eyebrows at my dad's shoddy attempt at impressing his guests. He clearly still had no idea where the nice china was, so the four tea cups were all mismatched mugs of different shapes and sizes. He brought out some biscuits and encouraged Sheri and Caiden to dunk the biscuits in the tea "as is traditional in England."

Dad had never dunked a biscuit in his life. If he had, he would have known that you don't give Rich Tea biscuits to someone inexperienced with the art of dunking, which encompassed most Americans. That was just asking for a "Code

Spoon" situation. At least let them get started on Hobnobs or Digestives as a practise run.

Fortunately Sheri rejected the offer of biscuits while Caiden just shoved one in his mouth without dunking. My father smiled awkwardly at him and sat down close to Sheri. *Very* close to Sheri as it turned out.

"Thank you both for coming today," my father began. Was he speaking to Sheri and Caiden? Or me and Caiden? "As you have both no doubt noticed..." he trailed off as he caught sight of the box of condoms. Caiden just stared at my father as if it were the most normal thing in the world to plonk a box of condoms down in a stranger's house. "As you have no doubt noticed, we have a big announcement to make here today."

He *was* talking to Caiden and me. The big announcement was coming from Dad *and* Sheri. I might have been a virgin as of just seven days ago, but I wasn't completely naive. Sheri's knee was nearly touching my dad's and the way they were angled towards each other meant I shouldn't have been surprised by what I was about to hear.

"Sheri and I," Dad said slowly, "have been spending a lot of time together recently and have grown rather fond of each other."

Oh God, don't say it. Don't say it. I glanced over at Caiden, hoping to see him looking as horrified as I felt, but he just smiled at me. He knows what's going on and he doesn't care. He thinks it's funny.

Sheri looked like she was about to speak next. The whole thing had clearly been rehearsed so that they could take turns. "Royston and I—" Sheri started, before Caiden interrupted.

"Your name's Royston?" Caiden asked, incredulously. "Fucking hell."

"Caiden," Sheri snapped. "Watch your language. Royston and I," she stared at Caiden, challenging him to make another comment, "are an item."

"I asked Sheri to marry me," Dad said, taking hold of Sheri's hand. "Much to my surprise and delight, she has agreed to do me the honour of becoming my wife."

"You're getting married?" I asked. Even though I had predicted what my dad had been about to say, actually hearing the words leave his mouth had been a shock, and my words sounded unusual as I asked the obvious question.

"Yes, dear," Dad said. He never called me 'dear' but apparently being nice to me was part of this new dynamic we would have to get used to.

"So we're all... family now?" I asked.

"Don't worry sweetie," Sheri said. "I have no intention of replacing Stephanie."

I didn't care about Sheri replacing my mother, because there was no way in hell she could ever do that. I admired Sheri and would probably grow close to her, but she wasn't my mum. As long as I kept in touch with Mum and spoke to her regularly, Sheri would never take that role from her.

Dad had been slowly removing all signs of Mum from the house anyway. All the old furniture that she loved and cared for while Dad was at work, was being replaced by new, modern pieces that felt out-of-place in our old home.

No, I didn't care about Sheri replacing my mum. What I cared about was sitting to the right of me. Caiden pursed his lips and blew me a kiss when Dad and Sheri weren't looking.

He was loving every minute of this. What's more, this news clearly hadn't come as a surprise to him. Caiden was the type of guy to take everything in his stride, but even with his reckless, carefree attitude, news as big as this should have come as a shock. But he knew. How long had he known for? Had he known when we slept together?

Caiden had been reluctant to sleep with me. That had come as a shock. He didn't have any standards as far as I could tell, and yet that night he had hesitated. Surely I couldn't be that repulsive?

I had a slim figure and even though my breasts were small they were at least pert. I got more than enough wolf whistles walking down the street to maintain some degree of confidence in my figure.

Had he hesitated because he didn't want to have sex with his new step-sister? Why the hell had he let this happen? I shivered and felt a sudden—and urgent—need to throw up. I didn't care about my dad marrying Sheri. I'd long since ceased caring about what Dad did. But Caiden as a step-brother? That was too much.

"Are you okay?" Sheri asked. "I know this can't have been easy for you to hear, but we didn't know how else to break the news. Your father wanted to tell you over the phone a few weeks ago, but I thought it would be better in person."

A few weeks ago. A few weeks ago would have been perfect. If I had known a few weeks ago I would never have slept with Caiden. I'd still be a virgin, but at least I wouldn't have slept with my... I couldn't even think it.

"Yeah, *sis*," Caiden said, drawing the short syllable out longer than I would have thought possible. "It's not that bad having me for a brother is it?"

Dad and Sheri were looking at me, so Caiden took the opportunity to bring his fingers close to his mouth in a V-shape before running his tongue between them.

I quickly crossed my legs as I thought back to that night as he buried his head between my legs and ran his tongue up and down my slit, exploring my folds before sucking gently on my clit.

It hadn't taken me long to come. I'd finished on his face and had seen the visible evidence of if as he came back up to kiss me. I made him wash his face first, because I'd been repulsed at the thought of tasting myself on him.

Now he was sat there reminding me of what he had done to his step-sister. He might have hesitated before agreeing to fuck me, but he'd obviously decided to go ahead and screw me anyway.

"Don't call me 'sis,' " I said, through gritted teeth.

Our living room was huge and yet right now it felt smaller than the dorm room I'd spent three years in and only just escaped. Blood rushed to my head as I struggled to focus. All the chairs in the room seemed to be squeezed together. Dad and Sheri were staring at me with concerned looks on their faces, but Caiden was just grinning.

"But you are my sister now," Caiden said. "Don't worry I'm sure we'll get to know each other and *come* to be best of friends."

I stood up on weak legs and the room came back into focus. Everyone was sat down calm and collected as they had been this entire time. I took a deep breath before speaking again. "I am not. Your fucking. Sister."

Dad screamed at me for my choice of words, but I heard Sheri tell him to lay off as I fled into the kitchen for a glass of water.

I can't be his sister, or stepsister, whatever it's called. I can't be, because if I'm his step-sister then that means he is my step-brother.

I quickly drank a glass of water which helped with the dizziness, but not with the reality of what just happened in the living room. No glass of water would change the fact that I had lost my virginity to my step-brother.

Chapter Three

CAIDEN

This is what happens when I break my own rules. The rules are there for a reason, but I'd gone and broken the most important rule of all. Rule number one. The golden rule. Never fuck virgins. If I had stuck to the rules none of this would have ever happened.

Admittedly, the virgin rule was not in place to avoid potentially fucking my future step-sister. I didn't fuck virgins because they got clingy. It was always the same. I could spot the virgins a mile off, but each one would insist they were different.

"No, I won't get like that, Caiden," one girl had pleaded when I'd been about to walk home without her. What was her name again? Naomi? "I just want to lose my virginity to someone who knows what they're doing. Show me a good time and you'll never hear from me again."

Bullshit. I hadn't been able to get rid of her the next morning and she kept conveniently showing up at the same places as me for weeks after. In the end, I invited her to my place and left the door unlocked to ensure she walked in on me balls-deep in some other girl I was screwing.

She'd fled my apartment crying when I asked if she wanted to join in. The last thing I heard was some whimpering comment about how she loved me. I felt a touch bad about that for a few moments, right up until I came all over the new girl's tits.

My 'no-virgins' rule had already been in place when Naomi added her notch to my bedpost, but my experience with her led me to bumping the rule up to number one. My golden rule. No virgins.

If I'd stuck by the golden rule then the introduction to my new step-father would have been a lot less painful. He'd still be an uptight dick, but at least I wouldn't have to look at him thinking about how I saw his daughter wince as she was penetrated for the first time.

I blame my decision last week on the toxic combination of alcohol, surprise, and a serious case of blue balls. Vicky caught me after a few drinks and I'd been so taken aback by her blunt proposal that I found myself thinking about it—or rather, my cock did—before I could remember my golden rule.

I'd also been a week without ejaculating which was almost a record for me. I hadn't gone that long since I was about thirteen. A bad cold had kept me locked up in the penthouse so I couldn't go out and get laid or hook up with any of my casual fuck buddies.

The temptation of masturbation had raised its purple head a few times, but I'd resisted. I liked to save up as big a load as possible for the next lucky lady. Better on some hot blonde's face than in a tissue. That was rule number two.

Considering all those factors, I didn't really have a choice but to fuck Vicky. Three times in one night. My cock made the decision immediately and it had taken just a few minutes for my brain to catch up. I took in the eighteen-year-old virgin in a buttoned up blouse and knee-length skirt standing in front of me; how could I resist?

Vicky had been a good fuck for a virgin. Hell, who am I kidding, she'd been a good fuck period. I'd assumed one fuck would be enough and that she would be too sore to go again, but she took me by surprise by rounds two and three later on. That girl must have watched a fair bit of porn because she knew how to ride a guy and get into the rhythm of it.

"I'm going to get a drink," I said, standing up and rearranging my pants to hide my erection. Now my cock was stiffening in my pants and pressing against the denim. That little sweetheart had me hard when she wasn't even in the room. "A real drink."

I walked into the kitchen to find Vicky splashing cold water on her face. At least she was as distraught by all this as I was. She certainly hadn't known this news was coming, so I could rule out her invitation for sex being some weird 'welcome to the family' thing.

"I do know how to get a woman all hot and bothered," I said, admiring her ass in her jeans. I hadn't fucked her from behind last week and I was beginning to regret the omission. There was a nice ass under those tight jeans. God only knows why she insisted on wearing boring, long skirts all the time.

"Piss off," she said quietly, not turning to face me.

The little angel never cussed, so saying 'fucking' in front of her father and then telling me to 'piss off' was a big deal for her.

"I'd take you a lot more seriously if you didn't sound like the Queen when you told me to 'piss off,' " I said, emphasizing the last words in my best English accent.

She finally turned round to glare at me. Her face was red like it had been that night except now she looked mad instead of in a post-orgasmic glow. Why did I keep thinking back to that night? Had it really been that memorable? She'd been a virgin for fuck's sake. How good could it have been?

"You knew," she snarled. "You knew didn't you?"

"Don't be ridiculous," I replied. She looked hot when she was angry. I wanted to turn her round and carry on where we left off a week ago. I looked around the kitchen and started opening cupboards until I found Roy's liquor cabinet.

"You can't drink anything from there," Vicky said. She leant over and shut the door, almost trapping my fingers inside. "That's daddy's alcohol. He won't want you drinking it."

"Daddy?" I said, laughing in her face. "You call him Daddy? Jesus Christ, you're such a child. Please tell me you are actually eighteen. I haven't fucked a minor have I?"

"Yes, I'm eighteen, pillock." *Pillock*? Was that another insult? I hadn't picked up on all the British terms yet. "Besides, the age of consent in England is sixteen. Don't worry, you won't be going to jail. Not unless it's a crime to be shit in bed."

I grabbed a hold of her hand which was still blocking my way to the liquor cabinet. "I could taste your essence on my lips for days after," I said, looking into her eyes. "You can say what you like about that night, but your pussy can't lie."

She yanked her hand free and headed towards the exit but stopped when she realized that would just lead back to the living room. She didn't want to be in there right now any more than I did.

I poured myself a large glass of scotch and took a sip. I added a few drops of water, but didn't add ice. This whisky deserved to be drunk straight.

"Daddy... Dad's going to be furious," she said. "That's about £30 of liquid you've poured into that glass."

"Well, I have to hand it to your dad. He has good taste. In alcohol anyway. Women, not so much."

"He married my mom," Vicky said. "If you knew her, you'd know his taste in women is just fine. Besides, he's marrying your mom and she's a remarkable woman."

I rolled my eyes and took another long sip of the whisky. This bottle wouldn't last long if I had to spend much more time around Vicky.

"Please don't tell me you're a fan of mother dearest?" I asked. The last thing I needed was another of Mom's adoring fans worshiping her every move.

"Of course I'm a fan," Vicky said. "I have all of her cookbooks." She motioned to a large collection of cookbooks in the corner of the kitchen. "Sheri's one of my favorite celebrity chefs."

"She's not a celebrity," I replied instantly. "She's an average cook who got lucky. And you shouldn't worship her. If you knew half the true story you wouldn't like her either."

"You're as ungrateful as you are immature. I bet she's given you everything you ever wanted and now you're just rebelling to prove how tough you are. It's pathetic."

"Sheri's done jack-shit for me except cause me no end of stress."

"Yeah? Who's paying for that London penthouse you've lived in these past few months? You know, the place with more whores going in and out than..."

"Than?"

"Than a whore house."

"Oh, good one. I don't know how I'm going to be able to match you in this battle of wits."

She grabbed her glass and refilled it with water. "Just leave me alone will you. This is tough enough for me without having the constant reminder of my big mistake last week staring me in the face."

Her big mistake? She couldn't have asked for a better first time than the one I had given her. How many virgins had sex three times the first night and came at least as often?

"Which time was the mistake, sweetheart? Was it when I ate your pussy? The first fuck? Second? Third?"

"Shut up," she yelled, pulling me away from the door to the far end of the kitchen. "Jesus, my dad is just through the door and so is your mom. Do you want them to know their children had sex?"

298

"I don't care," I lied. "Mom knows I like to spread the love around a bit. She'd be surprised if I *hadn't* fucked you."

"Well I'm not like that and my father thinks I'm still a virgin. I'd appreciate it staying that way for as long as possible."

"Is that why you dress like a virgin?" I asked. My fingers reached out and quickly opened the top button of her blouse with an experienced flick of my fingers. It wasn't enough to see any of those sweet, perky titties, but I felt my erection growing in my pants anyway.

What the hell was wrong with me? I couldn't see much more than her collarbone and I was already getting aroused.

"Don't touch me." She tried to sound mad, but she didn't do the button back up and made no attempt to push me away. She wanted me again. I could see it in her eyes.

"Do you think about me at night?" I asked. "When you're in bed naked?"

"No. Never."

She leaned back against the kitchen counter to create some space between us and pushed her tits towards me in the process. I could rip that blouse open and be sucking on those titties within seconds and she'd love it. That wasn't anger in her eyes; it was desire. She was fighting it, but I could see the passion there.

"You're lying," I said, leaning forward and whispering in ear. "I bet you lie in bed each night and think of me as your fingers move towards that tight wet pussy of yours. Tell me, do you prefer to rub your clit or stick your fingers inside your cunt?"

299

"You're disgusting," she said, turning her head to one side. She couldn't look at me anymore.

"I bet you're wet right now. God, I can practically smell your wet—"

I stopped talking when I heard a noise behind me, but I didn't move away. Vicky reacted quicker. She pushed me back to create a gap between us. I ended up standing right next to my drink which I picked up just in time for Roy to walk into the kitchen.

"What the hell is going on in here?" he yelled. I didn't know whether he meant my violation of his whisky or his daughter.

About the Author

Jessica Ashe is a twenty-seven year old British woman currently enjoying the much nicer weather found in Northern California. She enjoys writing about sophisticated and intelligent women and the hot alpha males that lust after them.

You can contact Jessica at author.jessicaashe@gmail.com, follow her on Twitter at @AsheRomance, and on Facebook.

30297623R00186

Made in the USA
San Bernardino, CA
11 February 2016